ISLAND INTRIGUE

After a bad bout of 'flu, Kathy Brandon agrees to spend three weeks, over the Christmas period, on the beautiful Mediterranean island of Majorca, with her Aunt Claudia. There, Kathy meets tall, handsome Miguel Lawrence, who she believes is the hotel's Assistant Manager. A restful holiday was what Kathy needed, but meeting Miguel and becoming caught up in mystery and intrigue were not what she expected.

Books by Sheila Holroyd
in the Linford Romance Library:

ALL FOR LOVE
THE FACE IN THE MIRROR
DISTANT LOVE
FLIGHT TO FREEDOM
FALSE ENCHANTMENT
RELUCTANT LOVE
GREEK ADVENTURE
IN SEARCH OF THE TRUTH
ON TRIAL

SHEILA HOLROYD

ISLAND INTRIGUE

Complete and Unabridged

LINFORD
Leicester

First published in Great Britain in 2002

First Linford Edition
published 2003

British Library CIP Data

Holroyd, Sheila
    Island intrigue.—Large print ed.—
Linford romance library
    1. Love stories
    2. Large type books
    I. Title
    823.9'14 [F]

    ISBN 1–84395–051–0

Published by
F. A. Thorpe (Publishing)
Anstey, Leicestershire

Set by Words & Graphics Ltd.
Anstey, Leicestershire
Printed and bound in Great Britain by
T. J. International Ltd., Padstow, Cornwall

This book is printed on acid-free paper

1

The stallholder held out the pretty little doll whilst fluffing out its miniature red satin skirt and pointed temptingly to the black lace which trimmed the ornate bodice.

'Yes,' Kathy Brandon said, smiling and nodding her bright head. 'I like it and I would like to buy it. How much is it?'

The man said something in rapid Spanish, at the same time indicating with shrugged shoulders and eyes turned up to heaven that the doll was the biggest bargain in the market that day.

'But how much is it?' Kathy repeated. 'Cuanto es?'

The man responded with more quick-fire Spanish.

In desperation, Kathy pulled some notes and coins from her purse and held out a handful of them to the stallholder.

'Just take what you want,' she told him.

A wide smile spread across his face and he put the doll down. As she watched him reach for the money, Kathy felt herself being moved aside gently but firmly.

'Un momentito, señor,' a voice said beside her.

The newcomer was tall, with straight black hair and dark eyes revealing that he was not one of the tourists searching for holiday souvenirs in that Majorcan market. He spoke rapidly to the stallholder in Spanish. The salesman scowled and seemed about to protest, then shrugged philosophically and started to wrap the doll up.

The newcomer turned to Kathy and looked at her rather coldly. He then spoke in English as fluent as his Spanish.

'The price is fifteen hundred pesetas which is about six pounds. It's a fair

2

price but may I suggest that in future you do not tempt a poor man by telling him to help himself to your money?'

He then turned away and vanished into the milling crowds before she had a chance to thank him.

Kathy handed the stallholder the exact money and, as she stood feeling grateful but foolish, her aunt bustled up to her.

'Have you seen the stall with all those gorgeous handbags? I think I might buy a black one.'

Her aunt's eyes fixed on the small parcel.

'What have you bought, Kathy?'

'A doll, a little flamenco dancer. I thought Richard's daughter might like it for her birthday next month.'

Aunt Claudia nodded.

'She'll love it. Now, let's see if we can find something pretty for your mother.'

With the determination of a born shopper, Aunt Claudia forced her way back to the stalls with Kathy following behind, clutching the doll.

Her thoughts turned to her rescuer. There had been something familiar about him. Where could she have seen him before?

An hour later, Kathy looked at her watch.

'We're late for the coach!' she exclaimed in horror.

Aunt Claudia, busily haggling over an embroidered tablecloth, gave her an impatient glance.

'A couple of minutes won't matter and I'm sure I can get the price down a bit more.'

She turned back to the woman displaying the tablecloth, but Kathy seized her by the arm.

'We're ten minutes late now!'

Reluctantly her aunt allowed herself to be led away, still casting wistful glances back over her shoulder at the tablecloths.

As they neared the rank of coaches, Kathy could see a figure in an orange and yellow striped blazer looking around rather anxiously. The driver was already in his seat and she could hear

4

that the engine was running.

Frantically she waved.

'Patrick, we're here!'

The young man in the vivid blazer saw her and his face lit up with relief as she and her aunt scrambled into the bus and fell into their seats under the disapproving eyes of the rest of the coach party.

'Everybody else managed to get back in time,' Kathy heard one woman mutter to her partner as the door closed and the coach moved smoothly away, but her aunt was too busy counting her parcels to notice.

'You should have got that black and gold top,' she said to her niece. 'You could have worn it on New Year's Eve.'

'I've already got something to wear, and I don't expect I'll stay up for the dance,' Kathy told her wearily.

Her aunt became heavily tactful and patted her arm.

'I understand,' she said. 'But you'll have to forget the past, Kathy, and look to the future.'

Kathy bit her lip. Her aunt was only trying to be kind and it was her own fault if Aunt Claudia thought she needed sympathy.

When they arrived back at the hotel, she hung behind for a moment to apologise to Patrick.

The holiday rep smiled forgivingly.

'There's always at least one person late and I knew I could rely on you to bring your aunt back eventually.'

Feeling better, she hurried after her aunt. Patrick was very nice but it was just such a pity he always had to wear that awful blazer!

After a snack lunch Kathy announced that she would have a siesta. Her aunt, busy touching up her lipstick ready for the afternoon's activities, thought this was a good idea.

'You still haven't got all your strength back, dear, and this morning probably tired you out. If you decide to come down later, I'll be in the lounge.'

'What are you doing today?' Kathy enquired.

'Ballroom dancing or bridge. I'm not sure which, but I like them both.'

After her aunt left, Kathy relaxed gratefully on her bed. The bad attack of flu she had suffered had left her with less energy than usual, but she was sure she would be fully recovered by the time the holiday ended, late on New Year's Day.

Her parents had been looking forward to the holiday of a lifetime; Christmas spent cruising on the Nile, when the flu had struck their daughter. A wan and listlessly convalescent Kathy, whose own holiday plans had collapsed, had assured her mother that she would be perfectly all right by herself at home, spending Christmas Day with her brother, Richard, and his young family.

'You're not fit to look after yourself yet, Kathy. I'd rather cancel the holiday than leave you here by yourself feeling lonely and unhappy,' her mother had stated.

Appalled, Kathy had refused to

accept such a sacrifice.

'You and Dad have been planning this trip all year. You'll make me feel dreadful if you don't go. I'll manage.'

In the end, her mother had made several long and mysterious telephone calls and had finally told her triumphantly that she had solved the problem.

'Your Aunt Claudia is going to Majorca for the end of the year and she said that she'd be glad of your company. Fortunately the holiday company were able to transfer the booking to a double room, so it's all arranged. You're going with her.'

The idea of three weeks on a sunny Mediterranean island had cheered Kathy up. She liked her aunt and was sure they would get on well. However, in reality, some snags had emerged. Her aunt had not, in fact, seemed eager to have a companion, and had referred darkly to 'emotional blackmail' on the part of Kathy's mother. The hotel, not far from the capital of Palma, was large, comfortable and well-run, but a survey of the dining-room on the first night had revealed that the average age of the guests was somewhere near seventy. Kathy had hoped for a few holiday-makers of her own age, but apparently the hotel was extremely popular with the elderly, many of whom came back year after year to spend Christmas and New Year there. Kathy realised that bridge, bingo and afternoon tea dances were likely to play a large part in this holiday.

An hour's sleep restored her energy but she did not feel ready to face the organised entertainment in the lounge and decided on a walk along the sea front. It was her first visit to Majorca and, although there were plenty of high-rise hotels and apartment blocks, she had been surprised by the beauty of the island. Now, wearing a jacket against the slight chill of the coming evening, she strode along by the sea, admiring the stark silhouette of the headland and the light of the declining sun on the tranquil water.

She was just about to turn back when she saw a figure approaching her laden with fishing rods and various canvas bags. It was Fred Deeds, who, at the age of nearly forty, insisted on viewing himself and Kathy as the younger generation among the hotel guests.

It was too late to pretend that she had not seen him and he hailed her loudly.

'Escaping from all the old ladies, Kathy?'

'I'm just enjoying the fresh air. I was about to go back.'

'Then I'll walk along with you.'

They started back to the hotel together. Fred was a self-employed builder, a bachelor who was devoted to fishing apparently to the exclusion of everything else. He told her that when the British winter curtailed his professional activities, he took the opportunity to come abroad and spend his time fishing from rocks and that sometimes he hired a local with a small boat to take him a little way out to sea.

He obviously enjoyed his fishing, his meals, and his evenings in the hotel bar, and Kathy reflected that he appeared to be a very contented man.

'What's tonight's entertainment?' Fred enquired.

'I think it's quiz night,' Kathy replied.

'That should suit a bright girl like you.'

She shook her head vigorously.

'No thanks! Everyone is so competitive! The prize may only be a bottle of wine, but I'd never be forgiven if I gave a wrong answer.'

When they got back to the hotel Kathy found her aunt in their room trying to decide which dress to wear for the evening.

'Is the black too formal for tonight?' she asked Kathy. 'I quite like the blue but I think Mrs Simmonds is going to wear her green again and I don't want to clash with her.'

'I think the blue suits your colouring,' Kathy said helpfully. 'I was going to wear my black skirt and top. Do you

11

really think that would be too formal?'

'Not on you,' her aunt said enviously. 'You're young enough to carry it off and it shows up your hair.'

Kathy ran her fingers through her copper hair which had been blown into an untidy cloud by the sea breeze.

'It'll take me ages to get it untangled,' she said ruefully.

At least she had the time. In fact, she was finding the daily routine of changing and preparing for the evening one of the more enjoyable aspects of the holiday. After the hectic pace of her working life in England it was fun to have the time to choose what to wear at leisure and then to enjoy a shower and apply her make-up carefully.

At seven-thirty Kathy and her aunt went to the dining-room together. The head waiter greeted them as old friends and led them to a table for four where two seats were already occupied.

Kathy had realised on the first evening in the hotel that her mother had indeed overstated Aunt Claudia's need for company. Her aunt had been greeted by several other ladies who proved to be old acquaintances. She had first met them on similar holidays and they had obviously arranged to holiday there at the same time.

Mrs Simmonds and Mrs Heswall were finishing their soup and were already eyeing the cold salads on the buffet. They greeted Aunt Claudia and Kathy cheerfully.

'How are you today, Kathy? Your aunt said you were very tired this afternoon.' Mrs Simmonds asked in a hushed voice she obviously considered suitable for addressing an invalid.

'I'm really am feeling fine now,' Kathy assured her.

Mrs Heswall, however, directed her greeting to Aunt Claudia.

'Only two more days to go now, Claudia,' she said coyly.

'Two days to what?' Kathy asked and was surprised to note that her aunt was blushing.

'Just a joke,' Aunt Claudia said rather

hurriedly, but Kathy saw that the three older women were exchanging what seemed to be conspiratorial glances. For all it was quite strange, Kathy decided she didn't care what their secret was so long as it didn't involve her.

As they enjoyed their meal, Aunt Claudia asked Kathy if she was intending to take part in the quiz and was barely unable to conceal her relief when Kathy said no.

'It's not that I don't want you to play,' her aunt said defensively. 'It's just that Patrick usually asks questions intended for our age group and you wouldn't know the answers to questions about Bing Crosby, for example.'

Kathy assured her that she understood and would be perfectly happy just listening.

In fact, she enjoyed being an onlooker, watching the desperate fight for the points which would win a prize and applauded delightedly when her aunt and her friends were duly rewarded with a bottle of wine and a box of almond sweets at half-time. As the older ladies settled down contentedly to consume their winnings there and then, Kathy looked casually round at the door. Her eyes widened at what she saw.

There was a tall man standing in the doorway, silhouetted against the light from the foyer. Surely she had seen that profile before? Was it the man who had come to her aid in the market?

Murmuring a vague excuse to her aunt, she rose and made for the door. He had gone by the time she got there but, after looking round the foyer, she saw him talking to the assistant manager at the reception desk. Although he was now dressed in a sober dark suit, she was sure it was the same man and as he turned away from the desk she spoke to him.

'Excuse me . . . '

He turned to her enquiringly, and she gave a small gasp of recognition.

'Of course! I remember now! I knew

this morning that I'd seen you before. I've seen you at reception. Aren't you one of the managers?'

He inclined his head politely.

'I have been at reception, but, as you can see, I am not wearing my lapel badge at the moment, which means I am off-duty. Can I get one of the other managers to help you?'

She shook her head.

'I don't need help. I wanted to thank you for what you did in the market this morning. I know I was being stupid by offering him a lot of money and telling him to help himself. I won't do that again.'

'It was no trouble. I'm glad I was able to help,' he assured her.

Having been thanked, he was already turning away, obviously expecting her to end the conversation and return to the lounge, but she felt stubbornly reluctant to do this.

'Please, I really am most grateful. As you are off-duty, can I buy you a drink?'

The dark eyebrows rose sharply but

then he smiled with what seemed to be real amusement.

'Miss Brandon, you are offending my masculine pride. I have a better idea. I will buy you a drink.'

'That doesn't seem fair,' she began, but soon stopped herself. She had the choice of letting an attractive young man buy her a drink or of returning to her aunt and her friends for the second half of the quiz. 'But I accept,' she finished firmly.

He led her to the small bar designed for those who wanted to escape the bustle of the lounge. At that moment it was almost deserted and he led her to a table in a corner, summoning the bartender with one imperious finger. Noting the speed with which the bartender came to take their order, she decided that her companion must be quite high in the hotel hierarchy.

He recommended a white wine to her and ordered a glass for himself. When it came, also at some speed, it was dry and refreshing, with a subtle hint of flowers.

'Incidentally, my name is Miguel Lawrence,' he told her.

'That doesn't sound completely Spanish,' she said cautiously.

'My mother is Spanish but my father is English, from Cheshire.'

'I see. And you know my name already. I suppose if you work here you learn most of the guests' names.'

'Not all of them, but we remember the names of people who come here frequently. Your aunt has been here twice before. In fact, she was here last Christmas. I remember you because of the colour of your hair. The manager asked the correct English word to describe it.'

'I trust you didn't say red,' Kathy said with feeling. 'I prefer to call it copper, but I hope the hotel staff don't know me as the girl with ginger hair.'

He shook his head.

'I told them it was the colour of a new penny,' he said simply.

She felt herself blushing and hoped that the subdued lighting hid the fact.

'I hope your health is getting better,' he commented.

'Do I look ill?' Kathy asked him with some surprise.

'Far from it, but I have heard your aunt talking to her friends.'

She thought of how she and everyone else talked freely about everything, either unaware of the staff within earshot or assuming that they did not speak English.

'I had a bad attack of flu, but I have completely recovered now.'

'I'm glad to hear it.'

He was leaning forward a little, clearly about to rise.

Kathy found that this was one conversation that she didn't want to end.

'I suppose you learn a lot about the guests from listening to them,' she said hurriedly.

'Oh yes, especially at meal times. The waiters hear some very strange things sometimes. And now, if you will excuse me, I have some work to do.'

She smiled, repeated her thanks for his help in the market, and watched him walk away. Suddenly an awful though struck her. Had the staff heard her aunt say anything else about her? But surely, even if her mother had told Aunt Claudia, her aunt wouldn't have told anyone else? She sank back into the depths of her chair, hoping against hope that if her aunt did know her secret, she had kept silent about it.

2

'We'd better make the most of today,' Kathy remarked to her aunt over breakfast. 'This will be the last of the quiet times. Tomorrow all the people who are coming for Christmas and New Year will arrive and the hotel will be completely full.'

'I'm well aware of that. In fact, I hope an old friend of mine will be coming.'

'Everybody here seems to know someone already,' Kathy said a little despondently. 'Perhaps there will be some younger people here for Christmas.'

'If so, they will be couples who won't want a third person tagging along or they'll have noisy families that you'll want to avoid,' her aunt commented a little tartly. She then looked repentant as she saw Kathy's face fall.

'I'm sorry, my dear. You must be

getting bored with all the elderly people staying here.'

'Not at all,' Kathy said politely, but her aunt wasn't listening.

'I wish you could meet someone your own age. Then you could go out together and I wouldn't feel guilty when I'm enjoying myself and you're not.'

'I am enjoying myself,' Kathy protested. 'I like Majorca. I like the sun and the flowers in December, and the hills and little farms we've seen from the coach. I feel much better than I did when I first came.'

Her aunt looked more than just a little relieved.

'What shall we do this morning?' Kathy asked her.

'Well, I've booked an appointment with the hairdresser at ten o'clock. Do you mind amusing yourself?'

So Kathy found herself with several hours by herself to fill. She wandered through the streets of the resort, peering in shop windows and occasionally going in to inspect the tempting exhibits. The trouble was that, in the past week, she had come to know the resort quite well and there was little new to see. She wished she could escape and explore the rest of the island. With this in mind, she bought a map and guide to Majorca, and on impulse added the Majorcan English language daily paper to her purchases. She then found a café and ordered a cappuccino, marvelling to herself that it was possible to sit in comfort at a table outside, in the sunshine, in mid-December.

She became aware of glances from more than one male enjoying a solitary morning coffee, and to deter any approaches she opened the paper and started to read, catching up on the news in England as well as topics of interest in Majorca. She noted a brief reference to the fact that the Majorcan police had arrested a couple on charges of trying to smuggle drugs. So, the idyllic holiday island had drug problems, just like so many European countries.

Kathy continued to read, noting the list of coming events for Christmas. Perhaps she and her aunt could go to one of the concerts being held in Palma. She could suggest it when she got back.

'May I join you?'

A voice broke her concentration.

She looked up. A young man in a sweater and jeans stood by her table, apparently so confident of her answer that he already had one hand on the back of a chair, ready to pull it out.

'I'm sorry,' Kathy said crisply. 'I'm waiting for my parents to join me.'

The newcomer laughed.

'Won't that be a long wait, Miss Brandon?'

Her eyes blazed with indignation as she prepared to deliver a blistering rebuff. Then she looked at him more carefully and broke into a welcoming smile.

'Patrick! Of course you can sit with me! I'm sorry, I didn't recognise you without your . . . '

'Without my blazer,' he finished for her.

'Well, it is rather noticeable.'

'That's why we wear them, of course. Any holidaymaker needing help or information can see that blazer a mile away.'

Patrick then pulled out a chair and sat down.

'Where's your aunt this morning?' he enquired.

'At the hairdresser's. In fact, I've just realised that this is the first time I've been out by myself since we arrived.'

'She must have decided you're well enough to look after yourself.'

'I had flu!' Kathy exclaimed impatiently. 'I admit it was a bad attack, but I'm over it now.' She bit her lip and then gave him a smile. 'I'm sorry to sound so ungrateful. She has looked after me well, but I'm not used to being dependent on other people and being looked after like a sick kitten can get a bit irritating.'

Patrick grinned broadly.

'Miss Brandon, you do not resemble a sick kitten in any shape or form.'

'If I can call you Patrick, you can call me Kathy,' she informed him. 'What is your surname, by the way?'

'Baird,' he told her, 'but when I'm working I'm so used to responding to Patrick that I almost forget I've got another name.'

'Do you like working as a holiday rep?' she asked curiously.

'It's exhausting, the hours are long and you never know what the next emergency will be, but it's never dull and I get paid to spend my time in places that other people have to pay to see.'

'How long have you been here?'

'Five months this time. I have worked on Majorca twice before, as well as working in Tunisia and Cyprus.' He leaned forward. 'The truth is, I love travelling. I work for a season, save my money, and then go off somewhere exotic. When the money runs out I come back to the holiday company.'

She thought about this. It sounded an alluring life.

'But what about the future? Are you going to do this indefinitely?'

He shrugged.

'A couple of years ago I would have said yes. But now I'm actually beginning to feel that I might like to settle down. My brother-in-law runs a travel agency in Brighton and he would like me to go and work with him. I might try it some time next year. We've had one or two nasty drug-related incidents this year, and I'm tired of spending hours in hospitals and police stations.'

She remembered the item in the newspaper, and saw that he was looking at her purchases.

'Are you interested in seeing the rest of Majorca?' he enquired, indicating the guidebook and map.

'I'd like to see something of the rest of the island. I was wondering about hiring a car for a couple of days. I have driven abroad before.'

'If you decide to do that, let me

know. We can arrange car hire with a reliable firm,' he said, and then she saw him look at his watch and frown.

'Time to put the yellow and orange stripes on again?' she asked, and he nodded reluctantly.

'I'm due back at the hotel in fifteen minutes to relieve Jane, the other rep,' he confirmed.

'If you give me a moment, I'll walk back with you.'

'No,' he said rather hastily and checked himself. 'I don't want to spoil your peaceful coffee break.' He hesitated. 'I have enjoyed meeting you off-duty, Kathy Brandon.'

She gazed after him as he walked away. He was a much nicer man than Miguel Lawrence had been off-duty, but, on the other hand, he did lack the good looks and strong personality of the hotel manager.

When she returned to the hotel she found her aunt in front of the mirror in their room, cautiously patting her hair.

'It looks good,' Kathy assured her.

'Are you sure? The tint isn't a little too bright, is it?'

Wondering what was the matter with her normally self-confident aunt, Kathy set about convincing her that the hairstyle did indeed suit her. Aunt Claudia might be sixty-three, she reflected, but she was still good-looking, always carefully groomed and plenty of healthy activity had kept her figure in trim and as lithe as many women several years younger.

'I had an idea while I was out this morning,' she said eagerly to her aunt. 'There are a lot of interesting places to see on the island. Let's hire a car tomorrow and I'll drive to the west coast. There are supposed to be some beautiful villages there.'

Aunt Claudia's hand grew still, and she gave Kathy a look almost of horror.

'Tomorrow? Oh, no, dear. I've planned to do something tomorrow.'

'Then what about the next day?'

Aunt Claudia looked a little flustered. 'I don't know. I'm not sure. Can't we leave it for a few days?'

'If you like,' Kathy said, vaguely hurt. Didn't her aunt think she could be trusted to drive safely?

The rest of the day followed the usual pattern: snack lunch, rest, down to the lounge to meet friends, and then change for dinner.

Just before they went in to the dining-room Kathy called at the reception desk to inform them that a light had failed in their room.

'I will get it repaired while you are at dinner,' the receptionist assured her. She was a tall, strikingly good-looking girl in her mid-twenties, and Kathy thought she would be much more attractive if she had not always been so cold and aloof. Her lapel badge stated that she was Elena Marquez, Assistant Manager.

'I haven't seen Mr Lawrence around today,' Kathy remarked chattily as the assistant manager made out a slip for the maintenance men. The Spanish girl lifted her head sharply and stared at her.

'I beg your pardon?'

'I was just saying that I hadn't seen Mr Lawrence in the hotel today. He's an assistant manager as well, isn't he? Is it his day off?'

Elena Marquez drew herself up to her full height.

'Mr Lawrence would not inform me of his movements and he is not an assistant manager.' She gestured at the plaque on the wall which announced that this hotel belonged to the Dee Hotel Group. 'Mr Lawrence is the son of Mr James Lawrence, who is the chairman and the largest stockholder of this chain of hotels. Mr Miguel Lawrence also works for the company and is here for a few days to inspect the hotel. I do not think he would like to hear himself called an assistant manager.'

Suitably crushed, Kathy left the reception area and followed her aunt into the dining-room. So Miguel Lawrence's family owned a large chunk of this hotel and several others! And she had offered to buy him a drink! Kathy was horrified.

Dinner was much the same as usual, though Aunt Claudia's thoughts seemed to be elsewhere and Mrs Simmonds and Mrs Heswall were being rather girlish and giggly over some secret they shared.

A singing trio were advertised to appear that evening but before the entertainment started Kathy went back to the foyer. The holiday company had its own desk, where a rep was always on duty in the evening. When Kathy approached the desk she found that tonight it was staffed by Jane.

The girl looked up, a bright professional smile on her lips.

'Can I help you?' she said politely.

'Is Patrick around by any chance?' Kathy enquired.

'I'm afraid not. Is there anything I can do to help you?'

'Not really. I was just feeling a little bored and I wondered whether Patrick would like to join me for a drink.'

Jane's smile stayed in place but her eyes grew decidedly unfriendly.

'I'm afraid that, even if he were here, he would have had to say no, Miss Brandon. The holiday representatives are not supposed to become socially involved with clients. The company prefers us to remain on the same terms with all clients rather than favour one or two.'

Kathy remembered how Patrick had avoided walking back to the hotel with her. Well, at least now she knew why, Kathy fumed as she went back to her aunt.

Returning strength was definitely making her impatient with her aunt's hotel-based routine, especially as she had spent some time that afternoon leafing through the guide to Majorca and deciding precisely where she would like to go.

She looked at the map again that night as she waited for her aunt to emerge from the bathroom. When she did, Kathy was waiting for her.

'Aunt Claudia, you remember you said you were going to be busy tomorrow, so we couldn't hire a car and go on an outing? Well, would you mind if I hired one and went exploring the island by myself?'

Taken aback, her aunt looked at her uncertainly.

'Do you think you could cope by yourself?'

'I don't see why not. Mary and I took turns in driving when we went to France last year, and I drove in America on that business trip.'

'Wouldn't it be too tiring for you?'

'Honestly, I've recovered. I feel fine! It would leave you free to do what you want without my tagging along with you.'

This last comment seemed to have a decided effect on Aunt Claudia as she climbed into her bed and settled herself against the pillows.

'It might be a good idea. Then we could both enjoy ourselves without worrying about the other.'

'Exactly!' Kathy said triumphantly.

'Only . . . shouldn't you have asked today if you want a car for tomorrow?'

Kathy's face fell and then she looked at her aunt with determination.

'If I ask as soon as we've had breakfast I'm sure Patrick will be able to get one for me.'

She spent another ten minutes happily making notes on the route she proposed to follow and fell asleep to dream of hilltops crowned by ancient monasteries and the sea beating at the foot of rocky cliffs.

Sadly, when the following morning came around, Kathy was a little disconcerted to find that, instead of Patrick, Jane was on duty again.

Determined to go ahead with her plans, Kathy quickly explained to Jane that she would like to hire a small car for at least one day, starting within the next couple of hours if possible.

'I know it's short notice, but I only thought of doing this last night,' she explained.

Jane's expression made it clear that she preferred clients who thought ahead, but patiently she reached for the telephone to call the care hire firm.

Kathy was lucky. The car hire firm had one small car free because another client had decided to upgrade to a bigger vehicle. It could be delivered at ten o'clock.

Kathy thanked Jane profusely and fled upstairs to collect her driving licence, passport, map and guide.

Her aunt was sitting at the dressing-table, gazing into the mirror, and scarcely seemed to hear as Kathy breathlessly told her that she had secured a car for the day.

'Good,' she said vaguely. 'Kathy, would you say I still look good for my age?'

Kathy stared at her, but grasped from her aunt's tone that the answer really mattered to her. She stood behind her aunt and peered at their reflections.

'Aunt Claudia, you've got beautiful bones, lovely blue eyes and it's always a pleasure to look at you.'

Her aunt swung round, kissed her, and laughed tremulously.

'Thank you, Kathy. I needed to hear that! Now, off you go and enjoy your day.'

'And you enjoy yours,' Kathy replied as she seized her jacket and opened the door.

'I hope so, I really do,' her aunt sighed.

Downstairs Kathy waited anxiously, but, on the spot of ten o'clock, a business-like young Spaniard arrived. Briskly he filled in the necessary forms, took the details of her licence and credit card, and then took her out to inspect the small hatchback that was hers for the day. It was similar to one she had driven before, and she assured him that she would have no trouble driving it.

He handed over the keys and she settled herself in the driving seat and switched on the ignition.

'Remember to keep the rental papers with you,' the young man reminded her through the open window. 'You have a full tank of petrol and you are fully insured. Enjoy yourself.'

When he had gone she spent a few minutes checking the controls, then unfurled her map and double-checked the route she meant to take. A sense of excitement was growing within her. She was free to roam the island and free to do what she liked. Of course it would have been pleasant to have a companion to share the experience with but she was determined to enjoy herself. Carefully she let in the clutch and pressed down on the accelerator.

3

It was a beautiful morning. A few fluffy white clouds drifted across the blue sky and the sunlight touched the high hills with gold. Kathy drove along the dual carriageway that led west feeling very smug and self-satisfied. She was aiming for Andraitx, an ancient town where a market was being held that day. She would stop there, browse round the stalls, have a coffee, and then drive along the west coast to Valldamosa, or possibly Puerto Soller.

Unfortunately, she was completely unaware of two things. The first was that many other people had also decided that it would be a pleasant outing to visit Andraitx on market day. The second was that Andraitx was an old town whose streets had been laid out in a time when donkey carts and mules had been the only mode of transport.

These facts were revealed to Kathy when she found herself one of a slow caravan of cars crawling through the painfully narrow main street. Parked cars reduced the driving space even further. Kathy began to wish she had gone somewhere else as she edged along, trying to avoid both the cars being driven in the other direction and the stationary vehicles on her side of the road. Halfway up the street a policeman was valiantly controlling the traffic at a crossroads. Up the hill, a hundred yards past him, Kathy could see where the street widened into a square. She began to hope that once she reached that, the worst would be over.

Just as this hope began to grow, she felt as if something was tugging at the side of her car. There was a deafening sound of impact, followed by the screech of torn metal, and the policeman stopped waving the traffic on and came running towards her.

Kathy realised that she had mis-judged the space to the right, the side nearest the pavement, and had hit one of the parked cars.

She closed her eyes and wished the world would go away.

The policeman quickly reached her side and began gesticulating angrily, pouring out a rapid fire of Spanish.

She shook her head weakly.

'English!' she croaked.

The policeman's shoulders sagged. He indicated that she should wind down her window and then, using sign language and occasional shouts, guided her into a side street. Here she turned off the engine and sat waiting miser-ably. In the space of a minute, two more policemen appeared. They walked her back to the main street and showed her a car with its back bumper torn off and lying in the road. This was apparently her handiwork. When they inspected her car, they found that it was unscathed, having apparently hooked the bumper at a critical point and neatly removed it without even scratching the paintwork of the hired car. Kathy gazed round nervously, dreading the appearance of a furious car owner.

One of the policeman spoke a little English. He asked her name and where she was staying, and then instructed her to get back in her car and follow another policeman to the police station a few hundred yards away.

Here, the market and the main street were simply background noises as a sergeant carefully filled out a form, copying details from the rental papers and looking at her disapprovingly over his spectacles. At his request, she was checking the details when the telephone on his desk rang. At first his answers to the caller were terse, but then he seemed to relax. He smiled and nodded as he spoke, and when he had put the receiver down he took Kathy to a waiting-room where she sat feeling very lonely and helpless. What was the penalty for damaging a car? Could she be charged with anything which would involve a court appearance? Her lively apprehensions had reached as far as wondering what Spanish prisons were like when the door opened and she looked up to see Miguel Lawrence striding into the room.

'So it is you! I was afraid it was,' he said resignedly.

She looked at him blankly.

'How did you know I was here? Who told you what happened?'

He smiled ruefully.

'I was driving along, looking forward to a restful day, when suddenly a traffic policeman saw me and signalled to me to stop. It turned out that he was someone I'd had dealings with before so he knew who I was. He told me that a client from one of our hotels, a girl with red hair, was at the police station after an accident. I came racing up here expecting to find someone surrounded by doctors and about to be carted off in an ambulance. Well, you don't look damaged, so would you please tell me what has happened?'

Kathy gave him a brief account of the episode, and then looked at him hopefully.

He sighed deeply.

'I'll go and speak to the sergeant.'

It was probably only twenty minutes before he returned, but it felt like hours.

The sergeant was with him and they were both smiling.

'It's all been taken care of. You're free to leave,' Miguel Lawrence announced, and she leapt to her feet.

The sergeant accompanied them to the front door where he wagged a reproving finger at Kathy and made a short speech which obviously meant, 'Don't do it again.'

Safely outside, Kathy turned to Lawrence for an explanation.

'The police have more important things to do than make a fuss over a minor traffic accident,' he told her. 'The car was badly parked and very old. When the driver comes back, the policeman will give him the details of the insurance company and they will pay for his car to be repaired. It will probably end up in better condition than it was before you hit it.'

He led the way down the steps to where her hatchback was parked near a sleek open sports car and held out her car keys.

'Here. Now you can get on your way. May I suggest you avoid Spanish markets in future?'

Kathy scarcely heard him. It had just dawned on her that there was no way that she would be able to get in that car and drive any further today. She felt rather shaky. She guessed it was a reaction to the accident and the fact that she wasn't in any trouble but she knew she could not get in the car.

'You don't feel like driving?'

There was an unexpected note of sympathy and understanding in his voice and she nodded dumbly.

He took out his mobile phone, dialled a number and spoke briefly before tucking it away again.

'Someone from the hire firm will come and collect the car from here. I said I would leave the keys with the police.'

She thanked him meekly as he stood frowning down at her.

'That just leaves the question of what to do with you. I suppose you'd better come with me.'

Her spirit revived a little as she heard the resignation in his tone.

'Thank you, but I shall take a taxi back to the hotel.'

'What will you do there? Tell your aunt that you crashed the car half an hour after you hired it? She'll feel responsible for letting you drive by yourself and it will ruin her day as well as yours.' His voice softened. 'Would you really prefer that to a day out with me?'

She lifted her head and her grey eyes met his dark ones. Finally she smiled wryly.

'I think that, on the whole, I'd rather

come with you.'

So a minute later, after the keys had been handed in, she found herself in the sports car rapidly leaving the town of Andraitx behind her.

'Rapidly' seemed to be the precise word to describe how Miguel Lawrence drove. His hands seemed to be resting gently on the wheel, but the car sped along the narrow roads.

Suddenly she saw a sheet of cobalt blue. They had reached the coast road, and Kathy, spotting the tree tops just visible over the nominal barrier to their left, realised that the road was really just a ledge constructed somehow between the soaring hills on the right and the precipitous cliffs plunging to the sea on their left. The road twisted and turned, following the contours of the hills, but the car did not slow down. Kathy gripped the edge of her seat tightly.

Eventually, the car drew smoothly into a minuscule parking space dug out of the hillside, and Miguel turned to Kathy.

'What do you think of the coastline?'

'Exciting,' she said carefully.

He smiled briefly, and then held out his hand to her.

'Come with me. I'll show you the view from the mirador.'

'What is the mirador?' she questioned as she got out of the car.

'The viewpoint, the lookout point,' he told her, pointing across the road at a stone staircase leading up to a tower.

They climbed the stairs and found themselves on a small terrace with a balustrade on one side. Kathy went to the balustrade and looked over, and her breath was taken away. The platform jutted out from the cliff and she felt as if she were hanging in mid-air. The view was stunning! Dark cliffs climbed from the sea. Here and there, trees clung to their sides. Ahead, as far as the eye could see, the Mediterranean rippled and shone, miniature fishing boats scarcely marking its immensity.

'They say that on a clear day you can see Barcelona,' Miguel said in her ear.

'What do you think of it?'

'It's marvellous! I never knew that Majorca was as beautiful as this,' she breathed, her eyes fixed on the splendour laid out before her. Then she heard the footsteps of another party clattering up the stone steps and reluctantly gave way to allow them room to look.

'Where are we going now?' she asked moments later as they returned to the car.

'To a house near the village of Deya. I have to speak to some people and then we will stay there for lunch.'

After a short drive Miguel turned the car off the coast road into a narrow lane, and within a hundred yards drove through the double gates in a high wall and drew up by a large house backing on to the hillside and facing out over the sea. Kathy noticed a discreet sign indicating that this was the Hotel Cygne.

When the car stopped a young man appeared, obviously ready to provide any help that was required by the new arrivals. When he saw Miguel Lawrence he grinned broadly and the two greeted each other in Spanish like old friends. Then the young man turned to the car, gave Kathy a rapid but obviously appreciative look, and turned back to Miguel. There was more Spanish, and the young man laughed and disappeared back into the hotel.

'Were you telling him about the incident in Andraitx?' Kathy asked suspiciously.

'Certainly not. I don't have to explain why I've got a pretty girl with me.'

Kathy followed him into the spacious, high-ceilinged entrance hall where brilliant rugs and pictures gave warmth to the dark wood floor and roof-beams and the white walls. Here, a man in his fifties greeted her companion with dignity and respect, but also with clear affection. Miguel turned to Kathy and drew her forward, saying something to the man as he did so, and receiving a nod in exchange.

'I've got some business to see to with the manager in his office, but it won't take long. If you don't mind, Ramon here will take you to the lounge, and you can sit there or on the sun terrace and he will bring you coffee.'

'I'd love a coffee,' Kathy said with feeling. 'And I don't mind waiting.'

He raised an eyebrow.

'I will try to make my business brief.'

Then he was gone, making for the stairway that swept down to the hall.

Kathy followed Ramon to a great room full of comfortable couches and deep armchairs. One end of the room was composed entirely of floor-to-ceiling windows through which Kathy could see a sun terrace. She made her way out on to the terrace where Ramon installed her in a sunny corner which was protected from the wind. The coffee arrived soon after and it was accompanied by a few tiny cakes.

It was actually almost an hour before Miguel was free to find her on the terrace. By then, she was leaning

51

against the cushioned back of her seat, gently dozing.

He stopped and looked down at her, inscrutable dark eyes following the gentle curves of her face and body, before he gave a polite cough.

Her eyelids fluttered open and she struggled to sit upright.

'I must apologise for the delay,' Miguel said. 'There were some urgent matters to be discussed and the manager is due at the airport within an hour.'

'There's no need to apologise,' she said sincerely. 'I think I have enjoyed just sitting here and looking at the view more than anything else I've done in Majorca so far.'

'I'm glad. It's one of my favourite spots. Now, the hotel is shut for guests until after Christmas, but the cook is preparing lunch for us and it will be ready in ten minutes in the dining-room. If you would like to freshen up, Ramon will show you the cloakroom.'

Kathy took the chance to waken

herself up a bit and afterwards Ramon led her into the dining-room. One table was set by the window and Miguel was waiting for her.

The young man who had been the first to greet them served them with a light lunch of fat asparagus followed by grilled fish, ending with a fruit tart. It was the kind of meal a family might have enjoyed using fresh local produce and was a long way from the bland international menu that Kathy's hotel found was most acceptable to its clients. They drank mineral water throughout the meal, but with their coffee came a small glasses of Spanish brandy. Kathy sipped it cautiously, but found it deliciously smooth, unlike the mass-produced product she had tasted at the hotel.

'Your two hotels on Majorca are very different,' she commented.

'We have four hotels,' he corrected her. 'We also have a very luxurious hotel in the old city of Palma. In fact, the hotel where you are staying and one we have on the Costa del Sol are the only two hotels we have that cater for mass tourism. Our other hotels are more up-market, like this one.'

'How long has this one belonged to your group?'

His face softened, and he smiled reminiscently as if he were recalling some happy memories.

'My father bought it about thirty-four years ago when he was still struggling to build up a small private group of hotels. He sold one decrepit, old building he owned in England at a good price to a firm that wanted the land and came to Majorca because he could see what an important destination it was becoming for English tourists.'

Miguel waved a hand vaguely in the direction of the rest of the building.

'This house and the land round it belonged to my mother's family for centuries, but when her father died she found that there was virtually no money left and that she would have to sell the house. My father was told that it was for sale so he came to see the estate, and she was waiting for him, ready to hate the man who was going to take her home from her. Instead, they fell in love.'

'At first sight?'

He smiled at her.

'Possibly at first sight, possibly at second or third sight . . . '

She looked into his dark eyes, half-hypnotised. His hand on the tabletop was very close to hers. Kathy shook her head to clear it and clasped her hands together in her lap.

'But he still turned the house into a hotel?'

'Yes, but with my mother advising him it became one of the first hotels to offer hospitality in a genuine Majorca country house together with all the luxury that our clients expect nowadays. Even my mother admits that the plumbing is a great improvement!'

'What do you do in the firm?'

He looked at her almost sternly.

'Well, first of all let me tell you that I do not owe my job to my father's influence. I trained in tourism and hotel management because I wanted to, but he wasn't prepared to employ me until he could be sure I was worth having as a worker. I worked for various hotels and travel companies for years, and when a post became vacant in my father's group I had to apply for it and be approved just like any other applicant. But I think both he and I were very proud when I was appointed.'

'And now?'

'At the moment I am what you would call a trouble-shooter. Sometimes managers want help to deal with local bureaucracy when they need an extension. Sometimes a manager makes a mistake and I will deal with the trouble it causes. Once I even had to deal with the aftermath of an earthquake. Fortunately, most of the time I just check that everything is running smoothly, show the personnel that they are appreciated and occasionally listen to one of them who has come up with a good idea.'

'What are you doing on Majorca now?'

His mouth twisted a little sourly.

'This time I'm trying to prevent trouble. Like so many other countries, Spain has a problem with drugs. Smugglers are bringing them into the country and are targeting the young-sters who come here for summer holidays and are ready to experiment more than they would do at home. Sometimes we find guests at the hotels have actually come to contact the smugglers and obtain supplies to sell on elsewhere. I'm spending quite a bit of time with hotel managers and the Guardia Civil, trying to think of ways to fight the curse of drugs.'

'Are the Guardia Civil the type of police I met this morning?'

There was a glimmer of real amuse-ment in the look he gave her.

'The gentlemen who dealt with your unfortunate accident this morning, my sweet, were wearing blue and white.

They are the Policia Municipal. The Guardia Civil wear green, and if you ever get involved with them then you will be in real trouble.'

Kathy gulped. This morning had been bad enough!

4

They fell silent for a while and the young man came to clear away the coffee and glasses. Once again, Kathy noted that their relationship appeared to be that of friends rather than employer and employee.

'Juan is Ramon's son,' Miguel told her after the waiter had gone. 'Ramon's family had worked for my mother's family for generations and everybody was delighted when they found that converting the house into an hotel meant secure work for those employed here already, and more jobs for many other people in the village. Unemployment has been a problem in some areas of Spain for a long time, and you can understand why some young people turn to drugs when they have nothing to do and have no way of planning a future for themselves.'

Kathy had remembered what he had said about the waiters at her hotel. She shifted nervously, and then squared her shoulders. She had to know.

'You said the other day that the waiters overhear a lot of interesting gossip, Mr Lawrence. Tell me, do you know if they ever heard my aunt saying anything about me?'

He looked at her warily.

'Firstly, I think we should be Miguel and Kathy to each other now. Secondly, what do you think they might have heard about you?'

She sighed in exasperation.

'You're not answering me. That means you have been told something.'

He looked down at the table, his fingers idly following the convoluted patterns formed by the grain of the olive wood.

'You should know that your aunt and her friends, Mrs Simmonds and Mrs Heswall, discuss their families a lot between themselves.'

'So what do the waiters say my aunt

told her friends about me?'

He abandoned his evasive tactics and looked at her.

'She said that she brought you here on holiday partly because you were recovering from an illness, but also because you have a broken heart.'

As her hands tightened on the arms of her seat and she seemed ready to leap to her feet, he added quickly. 'We agreed that it seemed unlikely that any man would leave a pretty girl like you.'

This only made matters worse.

'How many people know this? A dozen, all the staff of the hotel? Their families and friends?'

He shook his head.

'The water who overheard them is an old friend. He told me after he saw me having a drink with you, but I can assure you that he will never tell anybody else.'

Her cheeks were still scarlet with embarrassment.

'I didn't know Mother had told Aunt Claudia,' she said bitterly. 'My aunt did mention something about emotional blackmail. Mum was obviously making my aunt feel so sorry for me that she would agree to bring me on holiday.'

'Does it matter?' Miguel asked awkwardly. 'These things happen. You will get over it and meet someone else.'

Her grey eyes were full of anger as she swept back her copper hair.

'Don't pity me because it isn't true. I haven't got a broken heart!'

'So it is just your pride that has been hurt?'

Kathy gritted her teeth.

'Are you married?' she demanded.

'No!' came the emphatic reply.

'Good. Then perhaps I can make you understand. How old are you?'

'Thirty.'

'And you're not married. How often has your mother said that it was time you met a nice girl and settled down?'

He gave a quick laugh.

'Hundreds of times, I'm afraid.'

'What do you say to her?'

'I tell her that my job is taking up

most of my time and I haven't met the right girl yet.'

'And I suppose because you are a man she accepts that.'

'I think she's beginning to run out of patience. I am an only child and she wants grandchildren.'

'Well, I'm only twenty-three, but I'm a girl, and my mother is getting very impatient. She married very young, and, although she is always busy with voluntary work, she's never had a career and can't understand why I want one. Ever since I was eighteen she's been waiting for me to get married. I think she's already got the wedding planned down to the last little detail!'

'Don't you want to get married?'

'Yes, but when I meet someone I can't live without. Meanwhile I have a career I enjoy, and I like the freedom of being single, of being able to do what I like and spend my money on what I like. But I couldn't get Mother to accept this. In the end, I decided to make her happy by misleading her a little bit. I did a lot of work with a man named Derek, and we got on well together, but purely as friends. We used to go to the theatre occasionally or out for a meal. So, the next time my Mother started asking if I'd met anyone nice, I casually mentioned that I had been out with Derek a few times.

'Afterwards, all I had to do was mention Derek occasionally and you could see her wondering whether to order the wedding cake. Then, early in December, Derek finally got the job he'd been dreaming of. It was in America and I threw a big leaving-party for him because I was genuinely very pleased for him. I had quite a bit of holiday due and was planning to fly to Australia and visit some old friends over Christmas. Then the flu bug struck! I was in no state to travel and had to cancel my holiday. Mother came hurrying to nurse me and wondered why Derek wasn't at the door every day with chocolates and flowers, so I told her he'd gone to America. She immediately decided that I was suffering from a broken heart as well as flu, though I kept telling her I wasn't. The next thing I knew, she had arranged for Aunt Claudia to bring me to Majorca.'

As Miguel made a strange, stifled noise, she looked at him indignantly.

'Don't laugh! It would be bad enough to be the object of pity if I had been in love with Derek, but to be pitied when I wasn't is aggravating!'

Miguel threw back his head and laughed joyfully while she gave him a reproachful stare. Recovering, he hastily patted her hand.

'I understand, Kathy. Oh, how well I understand! Our mothers seem to have a lot in common.'

She managed to laugh at herself.

'It's just that I hate the fact that poor Aunt Claudia was persuaded to bring me under false pretences. We have always got on well, but somehow I feel on this holiday that really she'd rather not have brought me.'

Miguel gave her a glinting, sideways glance and she eyed him suspiciously.

'What's the matter?'

'Nothing,' he said airily. 'Anyway, you disapprove of hotel staff spreading gossip.'

Annoyingly, no matter how hard she pressed him, he refused to say any more.

The shadows were lengthening when they went back to the car. For the return journey, Miguel drove them inland between towering hills with edges so crisp that they looked as if they had been freshly chipped from some gigantic mountain.

Kathy craned her head to look at the view.

'Nobody tells you about this part of Majorca,' she reflected. 'The brochures show the hotels, the beaches and the bars, but this is so different.'

Miguel, negotiating a blind corner, nodded seriously.

'I know. I would like people to realise

how varied and lovely Majorca is but then I wonder if that would lead to quiet, beautiful areas like this attracting too many visitors. At least we have it to ourselves today.'

'To think it's Christmas in a week's time,' Kathy murmured. 'Will you be here then?'

'I fly to Barcelona tomorrow,' was his reply, and she felt vaguely disappointed, but he continued. 'I hope to be back here for Christmas Eve, so I will have a chance to visit Ramon and his son and the other people I have known since childhood. Then I should be here till the New Year.'

Satisfied, she relaxed in the leather seat, and soon she saw the silver glitter of the sea as they came down from the hills to the plain and made for the resort and Kathy's hotel.

Miguel became conscious of her growing tension.

'What's the matter now?' he demanded.

'It has just occurred to me that in a few minutes I'll have to explain to Aunt

Claudia exactly why I left in a rented car but came back with you.'

He thought hard for a while as they joined the coastal traffic.

'You could say that you had already given your car back to the rental firm. Let her assume it was back at the garage. Then you can say that I saw you and drove you back. It would be the truth, of a kind.'

She gave him a grateful smile.

'That is a good idea! It will save me an embarrassing explanation and there's no point in worrying Aunt Claudia unnecessarily, is there?'

In fact, Miguel dropped Kathy a discreet hundred yards from the hotel and she made a point of thanking him for his unexpected help.

'Even without that accident, I don't think I would have enjoyed the day much on my own, but as it is I've actually had a marvellous time.'

He smiled at her warmly.

'I thought it was going to be a dull business trip, but your company made it very pleasant. I hope I can get back from Barcelona before you leave.'

He drove away without a backward glance, otherwise he would have seen how she stood looking after him for some time.

Kathy had half-expected her aunt to be looking out for her anxiously but there was no sign of her as she went into the hotel. There were more people than usual in the lobby and a loud buzz of conversation. Obviously the latest planeload of guests had arrived. From now on the hotel would be full.

Her aunt was not in their room so, after a quick wash and change, Kathy went to look for her, wondering if she had met her friend.

She found her in a distant corner of the lounge, talking animatedly to a stranger, a man with white hair. She looked up as Kathy approached, and for an instant, her niece was sure she saw a shadow cross her face, as though her arrival was unwelcome for some reason. Then she was smiling again.

'Kathy! Did you have a good day?'

'Better than I expected,' Kathy said truthfully, her eyes on the stranger.

'Let me introduce you two,' Aunt Claudia said. 'This is David Evans, a friend of mine, and this is Kathy, my niece.'

The man rose and extended his hand. He was about six feet tall, with a handsome, sun-tanned face and, although he must have been in his late sixties, his neat blazer showed off a trim figure.

Kathy shook hands, and was surprised to notice that, although he uttered entirely appropriate words of greeting, his eyes were decidedly unfriendly. He was polite enough, though, and she discovered as they sat chatting that he had been at the hotel for the previous Christmas.

'That's when we first met,' her aunt explained.

Kathy was summoned to the usual table by Mrs Simmonds and Mrs Heswall as she entered the dining-room but when she looked round she realised that instead of following her, Aunt Claudia had taken a seat at a table for two with David Evans.

'You'd better join us, dear,' Mrs Heswall said placidly. 'It looks as if your aunt has decided she doesn't want our company this evening.'

The two ladies chatted amiably away but Kathy was thinking of her outing with Miguel and paid little attention until Mrs Simmonds nudged Mrs Heswall.

'Look at that,' she whispered to her friend.

Following the direction of her eyes, Kathy saw that the wine waiter was ceremoniously presenting a bottle of wine for Mr Evans' attention.

'That's one of the most expensive wines,' Mrs Heswall commented excitedly.

Kathy hoped that Mr Evans was paying for the wine.

Her mood was not improved when Fred Deeds airily assumed he would be welcome and took the spare seat at the table. For the rest of the meal he lectured them about fishing.

After dinner all of them met in the lounge but the singer who formed the evening's entertainment could not hold Kathy's attention and she found herself yawning hugely and apologised.

'I'm afraid the day was rather tiring,' she said. 'If you don't mind, I think I'll go and have an early night.'

Kathy was almost asleep when her aunt came up to their room. She seemed disinclined to talk and soon put the light out. Drowsily, Kathy thought it was surprising that her aunt had shown so little interest in Kathy's motoring adventure. Apparently her aunt was too preoccupied with Mr Evans. Vague memories of stories about lonely widows on holiday being preyed on by handsome bachelors stirred in her mind but her aunt was anything but a helpless little woman and Mr Evans was a bit old for a scheming Lothario.

The next day Kathy saw her aunt off

on an excursion to a monastery which she herself had decided would not appeal to her. Mr Evans appeared just before the coach left and took the seat next to Aunt Claudia.

'I hope that man doesn't think he's going to come everywhere with us,' Kathy murmured to Patrick, who had been counting the guests on to the coach.

He smiled down at her.

'I remember him from last year. He's a very nice man.'

'Yes, but two's company and three's a crowd.'

He gave her a long, enigmatic look.

'Perhaps that is what he's thinking, Kathy.'

At that moment Jane appeared at the door to summon him to deal with some problem and Kathy was left to puzzle over his remark.

At dinner that night the waiter had managed to fit an extra place at the table and David Evans joined the four women for dinner. Kathy had to admit that he did seem a very pleasant man, even though he still seemed to be eyeing her a little warily.

Patrick had told her that there were organised walks around the area and early the next morning Kathy joined a party of about a dozen tourists who were guided around the town and its surroundings. The walk involved fairly stiff climbs and Kathy returned feeling that she had definitely recovered from the flu bug.

The afternoon was spent in the indoor pool and, floating with her eyes closed, Kathy decided that this was perfect bliss.

Finally she went back to the bedroom to shower and wash her hair and was sitting in front of the mirror applying lipstick when her aunt reappeared. Her eyes were shining and she seemed to radiate happiness.

'Kathy, I've something to tell you. David and I are engaged to be married!'

Kathy dropped her lipstick and

stared at her aunt.

'Engaged? You can't be! You hardly know him.'

Her aunt sank into an armchair and gave Kathy with a dreamy smile.

'Oh, yes, I do. I met him in this hotel last year. I knew at once that he was someone special, and he told me afterwards that he felt the same. We've met several times during the last year and a month ago he asked me to marry him. I told him I wanted to think it over, and that I'd give him my answer when we met here for Christmas. As soon as I saw him I wanted to shout out 'Yes! Yes! I'll marry you.''

She seemed to come out of her happy dream for a moment and gave Kathy a sharp look.

'Aren't you going to congratulate me?'

'Of course, Aunt Claudia, if this is what you really want I hope you'll be very happy. But . . .'

'Yes?' Aunt Claudia enquired.

'But you loved Uncle Peter so much.

Are you sure you can love someone else?'

Aunt Claudia smiled sadly.

'I loved Peter very deeply but he died ten years ago and I can't spent the rest of my life mourning him. I love David in a different way, but I do love him very much indeed. David had a very happy marriage as well, but he loves me.'

Kathy brooded for a while, and then summoned up a smile for her aunt.

'I'm sorry. I just want you to be happy and if David is going to do that, then I'm glad! So, congratulations to the two of you!'

Aunt Claudia sniffed tearfully and managed to find a small handkerchief.

'I am happy, indeed I am, Kathy. My only regret is that we've wasted a year in deciding to marry, when we knew we would be happy together from the first moment we met!'

She leaned forward and patted Kathy on the knee.

'I know you've not been lucky in

love, Kathy. But believe me, you will get over it and you will meet someone who will make you happy.'

'Yes, Aunt Claudia,' Kathy said, only just restraining her desire to scream.

5

Kathy and her aunt went downstairs before dinner started. Aunt Claudia wanted to tell her friends her great news and she did not have to search hard for them. Mrs Simmonds and Mrs Heswall were hovering in the reception area, obviously waiting for her. When she saw them she simply nodded and stretched out her arms, and the three met in a tangle of congratulations and girlish giggles. Clearly they had been in Aunt Claudia's confidence.

Kathy, keeping apart from this, edged over to Patrick's desk.

'Aunt Claudia says she's engaged to David Evans,' she muttered urgently.

Patrick beamed.

'Well, Jane and I were expecting that, but we thought they might wait till Christmas.'

Kathy stared at him in reproachful amazement.

'You knew this might happen? And you didn't warn me?'

'We thought it best to leave it to your aunt to tell you,' Patrick said diplomatically, and then his smile broke out again. 'I am pleased for them. They make a good couple.'

Kathy sank down into the chair facing him.

'But it seems so peculiar,' she almost wailed. 'After all, they are both in their sixties, but they are behaving like people in their twenties.'

She received a rather disapproving stare.

'Look, Kathy, Jane and I have been travel representatives during the winter for a number of years. This means that the clients have been mostly retired people. Every season we have had at least four engagements, and then year after year we have the couples coming back, and I can tell you that they are some of the happiest people we have known.

'Remember, these people don't have the usual worries that can destroy relationships among younger people. They are financially secure, their families are off their hands, and they have the maturity to know whether someone will suit them as a partner. Believe me, I think your aunt and Mr Evans will be very happy, so go and join her friends and make this a happy night for her.'

Suitably chastened, Kathy rejoined her aunt and smiled steadily and when David appeared she was one of the first to greet him.

Dinner was a celebration. Aunt Claudia and her fiancé seemed to have an aura of happiness about them and, when it was time for dessert, a cake was presented to the table with a flourish by the head waiter. The surrounding diners who had found out what had happened echoed the message on the cake with an impromptu chorus of 'Congratulations!'

Kathy saw Patrick and Jane smiling

in the doorway and realised that they had organised this.

As the party left the dining-room, Kathy murmured some vague excuse and made for the telephone booths. Her parents were due to leave for Egypt the following day and she had to contact them as a matter of urgency.

'Mother!' she was announcing in a few seconds. 'Aunt Claudia has got engaged to someone called David Evans!'

She waited for the exclamations of dismay, the demands that she should persuade Aunt Claudia to behave more sensibly, but instead she got a delighted squeal.

'She has! He did come! Oh, I'm so pleased!'

'You mean you knew about this!' Kathy said in an outraged tone.

'Of course! She was afraid he might change his mind and not come to Majorca, but I knew he would! From what she said, he sounds perfect for her. What do you think?'

'He seems a very nice man,' Kathy said, and then her indignation burst forth. 'If you knew about him you should have warned me! It was a complete surprise and a great shock!'

Her mother's voice was apologetic and soothing.

'Well, dear, it didn't seem the time to tell you that someone else was expecting to get engaged when you were so unhappy about that young man who deserted you.'

Kathy bit her tongue as her mother continued.

'Anyway, you can understand now why it took a lot of persuasion to get your aunt to take you with her. Be tactful, my darling, and stay out of their way if you can.'

Kathy almost choked, and thought that it was fortunate for her mother that she was out of physical reach.

'Give them both our congratulations, and tell them your father and I want to meet David as soon as we get back from Egypt.'

Having agreed to do this, and having assured her mother that she herself was now in perfect health, Kathy put the telephone down.

She left the booth and, acting on impulse went to have a quick word with the head barman. She then went to join the happy group in the lounge. Aunt Claudia looked up at her a little warily, but Kathy smiled back at her reassuringly and saw her aunt relax.

'Mother and Father sent their congratulations,' she told the happy couple. 'They want to meet David as soon as possible.' She turned to the future groom. 'Incidentally, do I call you David or Uncle David?'

Holding his fiancée's hand, David Evans thought hard.

'I've always wanted some nephews and nieces, so I'll be delighted if I can be your Uncle David.'

Kathy bent low and kissed his cheek.

'Welcome to the family, Uncle David.'

Then she turned and signalled, and

waiters appeared with glasses and bottles of 'cava', the Spanish version of champagne.

'This is from the Brandon family, with their wishes for your happiness,' Kathy announced and the evening became a happy round of toasts and congratulations as more and more people heard the news and came up to wish the couple well.

Later that night, Kathy lay in bed and admitted to herself that she was at least a little jealous of her aunt. At twenty-three she still found it difficult to accept that romance was not only for the young. She was annoyed to find that when she did try to visualise the ideal couple it always seemed to include a tall dark man of about thirty with high cheekbones and dark eyes. She told herself not to be stupid.

She woke full of good resolutions, determined not to hang around Aunt Claudia and her new fiancé but as they left breakfast she found herself accosted by David himself.

'The weather is looking very pleasant, Kathy,' he said. 'I wondered if you'd like to join me for a walk along the promenade.'

She was puzzled but agreed and ten minutes later she had collected a light jacket and joined him at the door. They strolled along in silence for a minute, and she looked sideways at him, wondering when he was going to tell her why he had wanted her company.

Finally, striding along, his eyes looking straight ahead, he began to speak.

'You know, Kathy, neither your aunt nor I really have to get anyone's approval for our marriage.'

She murmured something tactful and meaningless but he carried on as if he had not heard her.

'However, we are both very fond of our families, and we hope that everyone will wish us well.'

Here he stopped, leant against the sea wall, and stared at her quite intently.

'When I found out that Claudia had brought you with her I was quite upset. I knew she had told your mother about me and it seemed to me that her family might have sent you so that you could inspect me and see if I was suitable.'

'No!' Kathy exclaimed. 'I knew nothing about you.'

'I know that now, but you are here and you are a representative of Claudia's family, so I would like to tell you what I want them all to know.' He took a deep breath. 'I love Claudia. You may see her just as an aunt, a woman past her first youth, but I see her as an extremely attractive woman and I love her very much. We've both been on our own for some time but we have thought matters over very carefully and discussed any difficulties that occurred to us and we have made up our minds that for us a life together will be one of happiness. To be practical, I am glad to say that I am comfortably off and I shall insist that Claudia keeps control of all her own money. I hope you will all accept both of us as a couple. If you disapprove, all I can say is that Claudia and I intend to spend the rest of our lives together anyway.'

He stopped, and Kathy stepped forward and kissed him.

'Uncle David, I think Aunt Claudia is a very lucky woman and I'm sure the rest of the family will agree with me. In fact, I only wish I could be so lucky!'

He looked at her with obvious relief, and took her hand.

'Someday you will be, Kathy, and I hope that day will come soon. Now, shall we sit down and have a coffee?'

The café they chose was covered with Christmas decorations. It seemed difficult to accept that Christmas was so near while the sun shone so warmly but the shops and restaurants were gaily decorated. Kathy knew that the Spanish traditions were different from those of Britain. The Spaniards had a festive meal on Christmas Eve and the gifts were brought by the Three Wise Men on January 6th. However, because it had so many British guests, the hotel did its best to combine the traditions of both countries. There was a special dinner on Christmas Eve, when the chef provided a splendid meal more obviously Spanish-influenced than usual. The notices outside the dining-room informed guests that there would also be a gala dinner on Christmas Day, to be followed by an evening of dancing.

'You will enjoy it,' Patrick assured Kathy when she returned to the hotel. 'The meal is always as good as a British Christmas dinner and the band is excellent.'

'I don't think that will be much use to me,' Kathy sighed. 'I'm not likely to be dancing with anyone under sixty.'

He shook his head firmly.

'On Christmas Day even the reps are expected to enjoy themselves. Will you save me a dance, Kathy?'

'Oh, but you don't have to! I wasn't hinting . . .'

He smiled down at her.

'But I want to dance with you.'

'Then I'll save you two dances.'

Aunt Claudia and Kathy both dressed with special care for the Christmas Day dinner. Aunt Claudia wore a long black and gold dress, while Kathy had brought a deep cream full-length jersey skirt and top.

David obviously approved of their outfits when they came downstairs. In fact, practically everyone had made an effort to dress up for the occasion, with the exception of Fred Deeds, who was wearing his usual sweatshirt and jeans.

'What's the point of dressing up?' he said defensively when he saw Aunt Claudia looking at him disapprovingly. 'I'm going out fishing as soon as the meal is over.'

'On Christmas Day?'

'Why not? It will be quiet and peaceful for once.'

As Patrick had promised, the meal was good and the band was excellent. Kathy danced with David and one or two other elderly gentlemen who proved to be expert dancers and obviously enjoyed showing off their skills and flirting mildly with a pretty young woman. She danced with Patrick, freed from his lurid jacket for once, and assured him that she was enjoying the evening.

'I'm glad,' he said simply as the music drew to a close. 'I want you to be happy, whatever has happened in the past.'

She realised suddenly that he might have heard some rumour about her alleged broken heart but before she could question him an elderly lady pounced on him eagerly.

'Patrick! I promised myself a dance with you, so don't refuse me!'

He murmured some polite remark, and gave in gracefully as the lady led him back to the dance floor.

It was some time later when he came to find Kathy who was in a corner snatching a brief rest from all the festivities.

'Can I claim my second dance?' he asked politely

Kathy rose but suddenly she heard a

very firm masculine voice behind her.

'Actually, señor, I believe this is my dance.'

Patrick was forgotten. Kathy turned slowly, unbelievingly, and found Miguel Lawrence smiling down at her. Wordlessly she moved towards him and he took her hand and led her on to the dance floor.

Kathy and Miguel danced together silently, conscious only of each other's closeness, until Miguel broke the spell.

'We have to speak sometime,' he said laughingly.

She felt like she was waking from a dream and drew away from him a little in order to survey him. The black and white of formal evening wear suited him.

'You are dressed up, aren't you?'

'Don't flatter yourself that this is for your benefit. I have already attended two other social events this evening.'

'But you still managed to fit this in?'

'I was determined to, though I only managed to get back from Barcelona late last night. Are you pleased to see me?'

She was delighted to see him, but refused to pander to his male vanity.

'Of course. There are now two men under sixty to dance with — you and Patrick.'

The put-down did not seem to upset him. He just laughed and clasped her closer once more.

The hours passed quickly after that. Kathy introduced Miguel to her aunt, who obviously found him charming and danced with him while Kathy sat with David.

Later, when the room was growing hot, Miguel led her outside and they danced on the paved area by the swimming pool as the music drifted softly to them. Then the band stopped playing and they heard cheering.

'Midnight,' Miguel murmured. 'Happy new day, Kathy Brandon.'

She lifted her face and he bent to kiss her lightly on the lips, then he drew her closer and kissed her again, more intensely, before suddenly holding her away from him.

'Kathy, I've got to go now. I've a plane to catch in two hours, but I will be back as soon as I possibly can be. I hope we'll see the New Year in together.'

Then he was gone, heels clicking on the stone surface. Kathy gazed after him, shaken and bewildered by the sudden change from her being in an embrace to solitude. She sank down on one of the seats by the pool, breathing deeply and tried to collect her thoughts.

'Be sensible,' she told herself. 'He is a very busy man, but he still found time to come and see you.'

After a few moments she rose and went back into the hotel, where her aunt and David greeted her cheerfully.

'Where's your young man?' her aunt demanded.

'Mr Lawrence, who is not my young man, had to catch a plane.'

'Then you can sit here and tell me about him. Where did you meet him?'

'Oh, he helped me when we went shopping in that market,' Kathy responded lightly. 'Then I met him here and discovered that his father is part of the management of the hotel chain.'

'How interesting!' was all that Aunt Claudia actually said, but Kathy could practically see a balloon above her head with the clear message, 'He's charming and good-looking, and his family is obviously well-off. Just the man to cure her broken heart!'

'Dear aunt,' Kathy thought, 'I haven't got a broken heart, but I am beginning to think that he might be the man for me!'

Boxing Day was inevitably an anticlimax. Kathy woke with a feeling of happiness and anticipation, only to realise that she did not know if Miguel would be able to keep his promise to see her again, and therefore she had nothing to look forward to. She immediately felt depressed and to confound matters her aunt was sleepy and reluctant to rise.

Kathy had breakfast in a virtually empty dining-room and then mooched around the grounds of the hotel feeling distinctly bad-tempered until her aunt finally came down and they went for a walk along the promenade to a snack bar when they enjoyed strong, hot coffee that finally revived them.

'When will you see Mr Lawrence again?' her aunt enquired.

'He said he would try to be back for the New Year, but that is all I know.'

Her aunt took another sip of coffee.

'So what are you planning to do till he reappears? I don't want to be nasty, Kathy, but David and I are just engaged and we don't always want a third person with us,' she said rather bluntly.

Kathy was slightly hurt but she managed a smile.

'Don't worry. I shall be very tactful. I quite like wandering about by myself and I'm planning to take the bus into Palma to do some sightseeing there.'

'Of course we both like your company

part of the time,' her aunt said anxiously.

'Believe me, I do understand, Aunt Claudia. I shall try to strike a balance between enjoying my own company and acting as a chaperone. Now, would you like another cup of coffee before we go back?'

6

Kathy had been surprised how easily she had fallen into the Spanish custom of a siesta after lunch and the Christmas Day celebrations had left her tired enough to sink easily into a restful sleep on Boxing Day afternoon. She awoke feeling like more exercise and, while her aunt slept on, she slipped out the door and down the stairs.

The hotel stood on a headland with the sea lapping the rocks below and Kathy walked along the promenade, settling into a rhythm that took her some distance along by the sea. The winter sun was already edging down to the horizon when she turned back. There were very few people about and she strode along happily until she was a few hundred yards from the hotel.

Ahead of her, by the sea wall, she could see a couple of figures and wondered idly who else had decided to watch the sunset over the sea. She then saw that the figures were facing each other, gesticulating, and she caught snatches of voices raised in anger. Suddenly, one of the figures broke away and ran along the promenade towards Kathy, forcing her to swerve to avoid being knocked over. She was aware of a dark-eyed young man with a set pale face who seemed completely unaware of her. It must be a lovers' quarrel, she decided, as she realised that the lone figure standing by the wall was a woman.

As she drew near, she saw that the woman was leaning against the wall, her hands over her face, sobbing harshly. Kathy recognised Elena Marquez, the assistant manager from the hotel and hesitated. Should she interfere? But she was too kind-hearted to just walk by this sad figure.

'Can I help?' she asked hesitantly.

The Spanish girl lifted her face and shook her head as she saw who had spoken.

'There is nothing you can do,' she said bitterly, and then collapsed into tears once again.

Kathy put her arm round her and the girl slumped against her, still sobbing. For a few minutes Kathy held her until the sobs lessened then the girl sat up and pulled out her handkerchief to mop her eyes and blow her nose.

'Thank you,' she muttered.

'Boyfriend trouble?' Kathy asked sympathetically.

'Not a boyfriend. My brother,' was Elena's terse response. She put her handkerchief away and stood up. 'You are very kind, but I will go back to the hotel now.'

Kathy surveyed the tear-stained, red-eyed face before her.

'I don't think that is a good idea,' she pronounced. 'You need some time to settle down and tidy your make-up. Let's go and have a drink.'

She led Elena across the road to a café. The proprietor, accustomed to English customers, produced a pot of tea for them.

Elena cradled a cup in her hands, her dark eyes gazing ahead apparently oblivious of Kathy.

'I don't know if you want to talk about your brother,' Kathy began awkwardly, and the dark eyes focused on her.

'I don't know. Perhaps it might help.' She drew a shuddering sigh. 'I feel so helpless!' She looked at Kathy. 'Have you got a brother?'

'One brother. He's a few years older than I am.'

'Has he ever caused your family trouble? Has he ever done anything of which your parents disapproved?'

Kathy thought, frowning slightly.

'There was a time, soon after he left university, when he decided he wanted to spend his life roaming the world, working when he had to and then moving on. My parents did worry for him.' She smiled. 'Then he met my sister-in-law. Now he's a happy husband and father and a college lecturer and my parents keep telling me I should be more like him.'

Elena looked at her wistfully.

'You sound as if you belong to a happy family. My mother died when I was twelve and I became the woman of the house and virtually brought up my brother, Juan, who is four years younger than I am. Then my father died when I was nineteen, soon after I started work at the hotel. Juan is clever and I was determined that he should have the chance to fulfil his potential. I have supported both of us but it has been difficult. Juan is at university now but he is not happy. He does not have much money and he resents having to take money from me, a woman.' Her long dark eyelashes were lowered. 'Perhaps he is a little weak as well. Anyway, he has been asking me for more money. Today, I told him that I couldn't give him any more. He told me that I had failed him and that I would be responsible for anything that happened to him.' The lashes lifted and the large dark eyes gazed drastically at Kathy.

'He wanted the money for drugs.'

Kathy leaned forward.

'Your brother was only trying to hurt you as a way of forcing you to give him more money. If he can't get money, he can't get drugs. You say he is intelligent. Maybe he will realise what he is doing to himself.'

They were only empty words but it was the only comfort she could offer and Elena looked at her gratefully.

'I suppose it is possible,' she agreed. 'Now I must get back to the hotel. I will be on duty soon.'

After a five-minute session with lipstick and comb, she looked fine and the two girls strolled back towards the hotel.

'I met Miguel Lawrence again last night,' Kathy said with careful casualness. 'He seems very pleasant.'

'Miguel is a nice man,' Elena said warmly. 'He works hard and demands efficiency but he can be understanding.'

'Couldn't he help your brother?'

'No! I dare not let anyone at the

hotel know that Juan is involved with drugs! They are very strict, very careful. If that went on my record it might mean trouble for me. I can't risk losing my job!'

Privately, Kathy doubted if Miguel would hold Elena responsible for her brother's actions but the Spanish girl was adamant that she would not seek help from him and swore Kathy to secrecy.

At the hotel door Elena paused briefly, took a deep breath, then walked briskly into the foyer, looking every inch the competent professional woman.

At breakfast the next morning, Kathy announced her intention to go into Palma for the day.

'I've looked it up in the guide book and it is full of things I'd like to see.'

'Do you think you'll be all right by yourself?' her aunt asked worriedly.

'Of course I will! It is a modern European city, after all. If I can cope with London I can cope with Palma!'

Later, as she made to leave for her

day out, Kathy heard her name called.

'Miss Brandon!'

It was Elena Marquez, smart in her immaculate uniform and bearing no resemblance to the tearful girl of the night before.

'I have been looking out for you. If you are going to explore the island, I happen to know that there is someone who would be happy to give you a lift and act as your guide.'

Kathy looked at her with sudden interest, and the Spanish girl smiled.

'He is waiting in his car, near the souvenir shop round the corner. You will know him.'

Kathy hurried out, turned the corner, and saw the familiar sports car with its dark-haired driver. He waved to her, and opened the passenger door as she reached him. The engine was already running.

'Elena called me on my mobile and said you were coming,' Miguel said smugly. 'I have rearranged all my appointments so that I could have a day with you.'

'I'm flattered, but why did you have to hide round the corner? Aren't staff supposed to go out with clients?' she asked, remembering Patrick.

'Something like that. Remember how gossip spreads. Anyway, now we have the day before us, what do you want to do?'

'I want to see Palma!' she said eagerly. 'I want to see the cathedral and the old streets of the city.'

'Palma needs more than a day to do it justice but at least I can show you the highlights.'

The coast road they took swept them into Palma and Miguel turned off to park in a large underground car park. They emerged to find themselves looking across a lake at the soaring bulk of the cathedral.

The day was wonderful.

They began with the best of tourist intentions, visiting the great cathedral, going on to the Royal Palace, and then visiting a museum. But gradually their cultural expedition became a gentle stroll round the beautiful city, with two young people happy to take note of interesting sights but basically most interested in each other. However, Kathy was sufficiently aware to register the fact that the city was not dedicated purely to tourism, like some other areas of Majorca, but was a living, changing entity. There was a sharp contrast between the bustling shops of the avenues which had replaced the walls that encircled the old city and the dark narrow lanes of the original town.

Later they strolled through the Plaza Mayor, a great pedestrianised square full of booths selling all kinds of craftwork. Beyond lay streets too narrow for cars, where shops displayed everything from tourist souvenirs to exquisite fashions. Kathy lingered enviously before one window, eyeing the single superb dress it displayed.

'I shouldn't go in there unless you are very, very rich,' Miguel cautioned her.

'Are there customers for such clothes in Majorca?'

'Indeed there are! When we drive back you must look at the harbour and see the yachts moored there.'

Reluctantly, Kathy abandoned the shop window.

'Personally, I think it's time for lunch,' her companion said firmly.

They had already had two coffees and nibbled on various pastries but Kathy was ready for a rest, if not a large meal. She had visions of a table on the sunny pavement where half of Palma seemed to be taking some form of refreshment but Miguel led her into a fish restaurant which was far too dignified to serve customers in the open air. In fact, Kathy realised that the cool interior was a far better place to relax than the dusty bustling street.

They ate plainly grilled fish whose appeal lay in its freshness and flavour, not needing the disguise of any sauce beyond melted butter. The vegetables were cooked but still firm, and the dry white wine was the perfect accompaniment.

They followed the fish with a fresh fruit and then coffee was served.

Kathy smiled happily at Miguel. She knew so little about him, yet she felt so comfortable with him.

'You seem completely Spanish to me,' she commented.

He laughed.

'Really? My Spanish friends all say that I am entirely English. I do admit my friends in England sometimes describe me as 'the Spaniard'. I suppose the people of each country notice what is unusual to them.'

'How do you see yourself? Spanish or English? Where do you feel most at home?'

He thought for about a minute, and then shrugged.

'That is surprisingly difficult to answer. I feel completely at home when I am in Spain because I have spent so much time here. My mother still has relatives here and she brought me to Majorca for most of my summer holidays when I was growing up but I have spent more time in England, and I love Cheshire, my father's county. I am lucky to have two countries but, I suppose if I were forced to choose, I would choose England. After all, I went to school there and that means that most of my friends are English. Anyway, I like unpredictable weather. Constant sunshine can get boring.'

'It would be nice for a time,' Kathy said wistfully. 'It is difficult to believe that this is midwinter and that soon I will be going back to cold England.'

'Do you like travelling?'

'Yes. I try to get abroad at least twice a year but, of course, the constraints of earning a living limit the time I can spend on holiday.'

'What is your job?'

'Public relations.' She lifted her chin, daring him to laugh. 'I don't deal with the glossy side of the business. I'm involved with careful, detailed market research and the statistics that emerge. For instance, I might go through the lists of clients at one of your hotels and find out where most of them come from and what the average age range is at different parts of the year. Then you could target your advertising at those areas, instead of wasting money in advertisements in the wrong place, and make sure those advertisements were aimed at the right age ranges.'

He nodded, obviously understanding what she was talking about.

'That is a constant problem. Advertising is essential for hotels but expensive and we know that a lot of it is ineffective. It's just difficult to find out what works.'

He glanced at his watch, saw that she noticed, and smiled wryly.

'I said I managed to get the day free, Kathy, but that is all. I have a meeting this evening, so I will have to take you back soon.'

Outside the restaurant, he took her hand as if it were the most natural thing in the world.

'If we cut down this street, we can walk along the seafront for a bit, and you can see the yachts before we head back to the car.'

The yachts crowded the harbour, gleaming with white paint and brass. Kathy was amazed to hear that some, which she had thought were ferries or cruisers, were in fact private yachts.

'Do you like fast boats as well as fast cars?' she enquired idly.

'Fortunately only fast cars. My mother was most upset when I got my first sports car. She tried to make me promise that I would never drive it at more than fifty miles an hour. My father was more practical. He insisted that I had proper training and instruction before I could drive it. My parents are very different.'

'But they are happy?'

He smiled and nodded emphatically.

'So love at first sight did last?'

'It did for them.'

Finally they turned towards the cathedral and, before they plunged into the underground car park, Kathy turned for one last look across the lake at the great building.

'I want to remember this,' she said wistfully. 'I don't know if I will ever come here again and I want to remember this view and the Plaza Real.'

'You will see them many times,' Miguel said, as if making her a promise.

As he drove the powerful car back along the coast road to the hotel, Kathy looked at him. He seemed to have suddenly become detached from her, unaware of her gaze, part of him guiding the car skilfully along, but part of him obviously elsewhere, possibly thinking ahead to his business meeting that evening.

Surreptitiously she watched the clear-cut serious profile until the car finally slowed to a stop. Looking round she saw that they were near the hotel, but not in view of it.

'Do you mind if I drop you here?' Miguel asked her. 'Then I can drive straight on instead of having to go through the back streets.'

Kathy got out and stood looking at

Miguel. He was already putting the car in gear when she spoke to him, hating herself for asking the question, but having to know.

'Shall I see you again before New Year's Eve?'

For a moment his face went carefully blank.

'I don't know, Kathy. I'm very busy. In fact, it may be difficult to make the New Year dance.'

She tried to hide her disappointment.

'Well, thank you for a lovely day.'

'My pleasure,' he said formally, and then the car was moving and he drove off without a backward glance.

It had been a lovely day, Kathy told herself angrily, so why was she standing there fighting back the tears?

7

Kathy simply told her aunt that Palma had been both beautiful and interesting. She didn't say anything about Miguel and, when her aunt remarked how quiet she was, she told her that walking round Palma had tired her out and said that she would go to bed early.

Kathy felt guilty at her lack of openness with her aunt but, if her aunt knew that she had spent the day with Miguel, Kathy would have had to explain how she knew him well enough to go out with him by telling her about the car accident. Kathy decided that at the moment she did not want to discuss Miguel with anybody else and she wanted to cherish the memory of their day together secretly. Her relationship with him was so undecided. At times she felt that he might prove to be the most important person in her life, while at others it seemed more likely that she would never see him again and he would dwindle into a holiday memory. Anyway, her aunt was obviously gloriously happy with David and Kathy did not want to bother her with her own unsatisfactory love life.

Her aunt insisted that Kathy took things quietly the following day but it turned out that Aunt Claudia had her own preoccupations. As Kathy came out of the bathroom the next morning she found her aunt impatiently thrusting garment after garment aside as she looked through every item in her wardrobe.

'Have you lost something?' her niece enquired.

'No. In fact I've just decided that I've never had it.'

She laughed apologetically at the look of bewilderment that Kathy gave her. 'I'm sorry. It's just that I've decided that I haven't got a dress that is good enough for New Year's Eve.'

'I thought you were going to wear the

one you wore on Christmas Day.'

'I know,' her aunt sighed. 'Now I can't help thinking that this New Year is going to see my life change completely. I'm going to marry David and move to his house. Nothing will be the same again. I know it sounds silly, but I want a really special dress to mark the occasion.'

'There were some beautiful dress shops in Palma,' Kathy said slowly, and aunt and niece looked at each other. Kathy had a fleeting vision of herself in a new dress dancing with Miguel.

'I'd like a new dress as well,' Kathy said decisively.

David refused point blank to come shopping for clothes, though he promised to admire whatever they came back with.

Aunt Claudia decided she did not feel like queuing for a bus and swept Kathy into a taxi and off to Palma.

The dress shops in Palma pleasantly impressed Aunt Claudia and she and Kathy investigated the stock of several

116

of them. Kathy was actually beginning to flag when they entered the bronze and glass doors of a discreetly expensive-looking shop. Here, at last they might find what they were looking for.

Aunt Claudia tried on a dusky pink dress which enhanced her colouring and flattered her figure. She turned this way and that, admiring herself in the long mirrors.

'Will it do, Kathy?' she enquired.

Kathy was enthusiastic.

'You look marvellous in it.'

Aunt Claudia took a final satisfied look in the mirrors.

'Yes, I think this is what I'm looking for.'

Then she asked the price, and was obviously taken aback when she found out how much perfection cost.

'I'll take it,' she said at last, producing her credit card. 'Have you found anything, Kathy?'

Kathy had been fingering a dress on the rails. It was soft and grey and glinted slightly.

'I like this but it is very expensive,' she commented sadly.

Aunt Claudia scrutinised it closely.

'The colour would suit you. At least try it on.'

When Kathy stepped out of the changing cubicle she became the focus of attention for her aunt, the two shop assistants and the manageress. The grey dress formed a column of silk chiffon that looked like grey smoke and the occasional silver thread in the fabric caught the light as she moved.

'Kathy, you look so beautiful!' her aunt sighed, her own dress forgotten. 'You've got to buy it! It was made for someone with your colouring.'

The shop assistants and manageress agreed enthusiastically but Kathy shook her head.

'It is much more than I normally pay for a dress.'

'But you have never had a dress like that. If you can't afford it, let me help.'

'Thank you but I have actually got the money. It just seems such a lot to pay for something I'll only wear a few times.'

'Listen, Kathy Brandon, that dress was meant for you. Buy it!' her aunt ordered, and Kathy obeyed.

They took another taxi back to the hotel, happily clutching the bags containing their dresses and quite exhausted by spending so much money.

Kathy's only other purchase that day was much smaller. Her aunt had forgotten to buy the local English newspaper and the hotel had sold out.

'I'll get you a copy from that newsagent's near the shoe shop,' Kathy volunteered.

'Would you, dear? I know it's silly, but I do like to know what's going on back in England and I miss the crossword.'

The newsagent had one copy of paper left, so Kathy bought it, tucked it under her arm and started on the short walk back to the hotel. Her head was full of visions of herself in her new dress and she was startled when a familiar voice sounded behind her.

'Homesick for England? I never look at a paper till I get back.'

It was Fred Deeds, draped with fishing gear as usual. Kathy did not particularly like the man but politeness forced her to smile and let him fall into step beside her.

'Are you going fishing or coming back?'

'Coming back,' he replied, patting the plastic container he carried. 'I've got what I wanted today.'

He was smiling to himself, as though gloating over some secret and Kathy felt an instinctive distrust.

'I thought you always went out at night?'

'Usually,' he said tersely and did not volunteer any more information.

They found an unusual amount of bustle going on at the hotel entrance.

'What's happening?' Kathy asked Mrs Heswall, who was busy telling something to Mrs Simmonds.

'The police are here!' said her aunt's

friend. 'I don't know why but they are all armed. It must be something serious.'

Kathy hesitated, automatically experiencing feelings of guilt as she remembered her car accident but her companion had come to a complete halt.

'What colour are their uniforms?' he demanded.

'Olive green. Somebody said they are the Guardia Civil.'

'Then someone is in trouble,' Fred commented and suddenly thrust the plastic container at Kathy. 'Here, take this.'

She had to take it or let it fall though it was unexpectedly heavy. Before she could say anything, Deeds had linked his arm through hers and was walking her rapidly through the door and across the foyer to the lifts, his body screening her and what she carried from the four burly men in uniform who were by the reception desk.

Kathy saw them, and then forgot

them completely, for behind the reception desk was Miguel. He was dressed in the formal dark suit of a manager and was talking to the police.

Kathy's face lit up, and at that moment he lifted his head and saw her by the side of Fred Deeds. She smiled at him, and waited for his response, but his face did not change or show any sign of recognition. His gaze passed on and he turned back to the man he had been speaking to.

Kathy was hardly aware of Fred almost pushing her into the lift and pressing the button. Miguel had seen her, she knew, but he had ignored her.

'This is where I get out,' Fred murmured, taking the plastic case from her lax grip, and then he vanished. She pressed the button for her own floor and, like an automaton, she went to her room and delivered the paper to her aunt.

There must have been some explanation for Miguel's behaviour, she found herself thinking. Perhaps the presence of the police had meant trouble for the hotel. He had been fully occupied by the problem and it had been an inopportune moment to contact him. Surely he could at least have acknowledged her existence somehow!

Some time later her aunt wondered aloud about some details of the New Year's Eve celebrations and Kathy seized on this as an excuse to go downstairs to ask at reception.

'There's no need to do that,' her aunt said. 'I'm going down myself to meet David in a few minutes.'

'It's no trouble at all,' Kathy assured her. 'I can check easily on my way to the lounge and then we will all meet there.'

Her heart was beating uncomfortably as she made her way down. She had to see Miguel again and find out whether the way he had ignored her had been deliberate or not.

She was to be disappointed. The police had gone, and so had Miguel. Elena Marquez was now in charge of reception.

Kathy went over to see her and, as she drew closer, she was shocked at the other girl's appearance. Elena was as immaculately groomed as ever but her face was paper-white and there were shadows like bruises under her eyes.

'What's the matter?' Kathy asked. 'Hasn't your brother come back?'

Elena looked as if it was taking a great effort to stop herself breaking down. When Kathy spoke to her, Elena's hands began to shake and she gripped the edge of the counter to control them.

'Juan came back yesterday,' she said slowly.

'Did he ask you for money again?'

'No. He was angry, very angry, but not with me.' She looked at Kathy tragically. 'Two friends of his had been taking drugs. They started fighting each other. One of them stabbed the other and killed him. Afterwards, when he realised what he had done, he killed himself.' She closed her eyes as Kathy stared at her, appalled. 'Now Juan says that the drug sellers are the real murderers and that he knows who is responsible for bringing a lot of drugs into Majorca. He said that he is going to kill him to avenge his friends.'

She was trembling all over now.

'I have tried to find him. I have contacted all his friends that I know and asked them to tell me if they see him. I cannot lose him! He is all I have!'

'You'll have to go to the police and tell them this!' Kathy exclaimed.

'Perhaps. But if I do that and it was just his hurt and anger talking, I will have involved him with the police and made it known that he has been taking drugs. I must think of something else.'

'He is young after all,' Kathy tried to reassure her. 'Young men often say they are going to do something stupid and then think better of it. Your brother will be back to see you soon.'

'I hope so.'

Abruptly Elena deserted the counter, hurrying through the door behind it and slamming it closed. Kathy hesitated for a while, and then drifted away to the lounge, but her aunt and David did not appear, and she came out again with the vague idea of looking for them.

Elena had not returned to the reception counter. Instead Miguel stood there alone.

Kathy took a deep breath and walked towards him. She wasn't sure what to say, but he solved the problem for her.

'Can I help you, Miss Brandon?'

His cool, polite voice was like a slap in the face. It was clear that there had been no mistake earlier. For some reason he had decided that the relationship that had been growing between them had to be destroyed. She looked round, wondering if anybody could see how humiliated she felt, but the few guests about, such as Fred Deeds, were making towards the lounge and were happily unaware of the situation at the desk.

Kathy resolved that she would at least preserve her dignity. She would not ask him why he was behaving like this.

Instead, she heard herself putting her aunt's query to him and received the answer with a little nod of acknowledgement. Then she turned around and went back to the lounge, where she found that Aunt Claudia and David had just arrived.

Kathy found it difficult to get through the rest of the evening. Fortunately both Mrs Simmonds and Mrs Heswall had also been shopping, though only for small items in the local shops, and Aunt Claudia and her friends had plenty to talk about while David half-listened and regarded his fiancée with undisguised pleasure and affection.

After a while, Kathy slipped away unobtrusively and made her way out to the swimming pool where she found a sheltered spot on one of the seats that were used by sunbathers during the day.

The day had begun so well and she had been so hopeful when she bought the grey dress that she would be wearing it on New Year's Eve while Miguel held her in his arms.

What had gone wrong? She asked herself the question again and again. It could not have been the presence of the police, for there had been no sign of them later when he had addressed her so formally. He might have wanted to avoid staff gossip, but he could at least have smiled. Instead his behaviour had been icy.

She thought back over the few days since she had met him. Their first meeting had shown her as being rather foolish and that same evening he had displayed nothing but cool politeness. He had rescued her from the consequences of her accident with the car, but presumably he saw that as part of his responsibility to his clients. Had it meant anything to him that the day had afterwards turned out to be so pleasant? Perhaps that had been mere politeness again. At the Christmas Dance she had been one of the few unattached women under sixty and he might have preferred her to the alternatives. He had kissed her, but then what man would have refused the chance to kiss a young girl who was obviously impressed by him. Perhaps he had seen her boast of an unbroken heart as a challenge and had deliberately set out to attract her, to show her she was not invulnerable.

There was still the day in Palma. He had gone to some trouble to get the message to her through Elena, and that was after rearranging his business affairs. Or was it? She only had his word for it that he had had to make a great effort to get the day free to be with her. Unseen, she blushed furiously. She had been so flattered that she had not questioned what he told her. In reality he might have found himself with an empty day and decided to amuse himself with her for a few more hours.

Now, for some reason, he no longer wanted to flirt with her or to enjoy her admiration. The relationship had become an embarrassment, a nuisance and he had rapidly put an end to it. Perhaps someone had pointed out that the heir to a large part of a hotel empire should not get too involved with one of the guests and that it was unfitting and below his dignity. Perhaps he already had a girlfriend and had learned that she would soon appear on the scene. Whatever the reason, the dreams that Kathy admitted she had begun to weave about him would have to be forgotten. She gave a long sigh.

'There you are!' she heard moments later.

It was Aunt Claudia. 'David said he was sure he'd seen you through the window. What are you doing out here on your own?'

'Thinking,' Kathy said a little dolefully.

Her aunt, protected against the night air by a warm cardigan, sat down beside her.

'You've been quiet all evening. Don't think I didn't notice. What's the matter?'

'I was thinking that in a couple of days we will be back in England.'

'Does that make you sad?'

'I don't know. I've enjoyed Majorca very much. I like the island itself, the people and the sunshine, and physically I feel much better but I think I feel like getting back to work again.'

'You're ready to face the world?'

'The familiar world I know and can cope with.'

'Good. You can't go on brooding for ever over some silly young man who didn't appreciate you.'

Kathy tensed. How did her aunt know? Then she realised that Aunt Claudia was thinking of Derek and not Miguel.

'I envy you, Aunt Claudia. David is a lovely man. I wish I could find someone like him.'

Her aunt laughed like a young girl.

'I've had a lot more years than you to find my ideal man. I've been very lucky — I found two.' She put her arm round Kathy's shoulders and hugged her sympathetically. 'Don't worry. You'll find someone to love who will love you in return and it will probably be when you least expect it. I met my first husband in a bookshop when I took the last copy of a book he wanted just as he was about to pick it up. He asked me if I really wanted it and I told him that of course I did and then we got talking.'

She stood up firmly.

'It's getting too cold for me out here. Let's go and have a night-cap and then go to bed.'

8

There were only two full days left before they flew back to England. Kathy found she was indeed looking forward to getting back to some hard work which might help her forget Miguel, but she was determined that she was not going to let his strange behaviour spoil what remained of the holiday. She should have remembered the short life and unhappy endings of most holiday romances.

On December 30th, she climbed into a coach along with her aunt and other guests for a tour of some of the scenic splendours of Majorca, a tour which took them through some of the beautiful inland country to a high rocky headland with precipitous cliffs. Happily, she abandoned herself to being a tourist, buying souvenirs recklessly at every stop while her aunt tried to photograph every scenic spot, then bought a fresh reel of film when she ran out and used that up as well.

'Will you remember what you've photographed?' Kathy asked and her aunt laughed happily.

'This is a very special holiday for me, remember. I want as much as possible to remind me of it in the years to come.'

Kathy felt a pang of envy, and was immediately ashamed of herself. She should be glad that Aunt Claudia and David had found new partners. One young man who had disappointed her did not have the right to blight her whole life.

They returned to the hotel in the late afternoon, happily tired and snatched a rest before dinner. After the meal, they went out to a bar which David had discovered in their absence and experimented with some exotic cocktails before going back to an early bed.

Kathy woke early on New Year's Eve and heard her aunt yawn as she

134

stretched out one hand for the clock.

'Seven-thirty. What's the weather like for our last full day?'

Kathy slipped out of bed and pulled back the heavy curtains. Sunlight flooded into the room.

'Perfect. The sky is blue and the sun is shining on the hills and the sea. It's time for us to get up.'

'It's going to be a long day,' Aunt Claudia protested, snuggling down in her bed again.

'It's our last full day in Majorca and we don't want to miss any of it.'

By the time Kathy had showered and dressed her aunt had roused herself. The dining-room was still comparatively empty when they went down to breakfast and Aunt Claudia helped herself generously.

'I don't expect we'll feel like eating much tomorrow morning,' she observed. 'This is our last chance to have a cooked breakfast which someone else has prepared. After this, it's back to cereals and toast.'

After breakfast she insisted that they sorted things out and do at least a little packing.

'We have to leave our room by twelve tomorrow, and we might well sleep till nearly that time,' she insisted when Kathy wailed that there were better things to do, so her niece obediently half-filled her suitcase. Then, like her aunt, she checked whether she had presents enough for her family, and found that although she had plenty of goodies for her little niece she had nothing for her sister-in-law.

'I could get her that book of photographs of Majorca that we saw in the newsagent's,' she brooded.

'What a good idea,' Aunt Claudia agreed. 'I know they are thinking of coming to Majorca themselves some time.'

Leaving her aunt with David, Kathy set off for the shop. Although the day was clear and bright there was a cool wind and she hurried along on her errand, sparing a glance for the sun glittering on the water. She bought the book and turned back.

Near the hotel, she was passing through a narrow passageway between some shops when someone coming the other way brushed against her as she looked in a window. She looked up, startled, and saw a haggard, unshaven young man. She recognised him as Juan Marquez, Elena's brother.

'He must be going to the hotel to find her,' Kathy guessed. 'Perhaps he's calmed down and come to make his peace with his sister. That will make her happier, at any rate, though he does look as if he needs some food and a good bath.'

At least the old year would be ending well for Elena, and Kathy returned to the hotel very satisfied with her excursion and busied herself with minor matters until David insisted on whisking her and her aunt off for lunch at a restaurant overlooking the sea.

'I know you usually have a snack lunch in your room or a café,' he told them, 'but we are having a late dinner so we need a proper meal to keep us going. Anyway,' he said with a sudden youthful grin, 'I feel like celebrating all day.'

After the meal and some wine it was siesta time. Kathy woke up full of restless energy. Sitting in the lounge till it was time to dress for dinner did not appeal to her. She decided that she would go for a walk instead.

It was growing colder as the sun sank down, and Kathy was glad of her warm jacket. Still, in a little more than twenty-four hours she would be shivering in England. She strode out briskly, keeping near the sea as much as possible, aiming for a rocky headland topped by pine trees. When she reached it she stood on the top for a while, watching as the sun sank even lower. It seemed appropriate that the passing of the last day of the old year was marked by such a splendid sunset.

Then some faint noise caught her attention. Moving quietly forward, she peered over the rocky crest. Below her a man in dark casual clothes was sitting on a flat rock and gazing out to sea. Was someone else saying goodbye to Majorca? The man shifted a little and moved his head and she saw that it was Miguel.

Perhaps she gasped or perhaps he saw a movement for he was suddenly on his feet in one smooth movement and staring up at her. There was still light enough for her to see his expression change to amazed delight. She heard him call her name but she turned and ran back along the headland and along the footpath to the road. There she slowed down and looked over her shoulder. There seemed to be no sign of Miguel. He had not followed her.

She hurried towards the distant bulk of the hotel, angry with herself and with Miguel. Why had she turned and run like a scared schoolgirl? Why had he been so cold to her the other day, when she had seen by this first instinctive reaction at the sight of her that his feelings were as strong as hers? Why hadn't he followed her? What external constraints were forcing him to behave as if they were strangers?

She was waiting for the lift, thoughts disorganised and heart beating fast, when Fred strolled up and stood waiting beside her. Politeness made her acknowledge his presence when he smiled at her but she had been wary of him ever since his behaviour when the police had been at the hotel.

A couple of elderly ladies greeted him more warmly.

'We hope you are going to be here for the dinner and the dance, Mr Deeds. It will be worth giving up your fishing for once.'

Deeds grinned and shook his head.

'I'm having a meal with a Spanish friend of mine, not here. Then I'll fit in a little fishing. I was going to stay on the boat all night but my plans have changed. I'll be back in time to see you eat your twelve grapes at midnight.

Keep me a dance.'

Kathy found her aunt in their room, comfortably wrapped in a dressing-gown and reading a magazine which she put down as her niece appeared.

'I was beginning to wonder where you had got to,' she observed, and then peered at Kathy closely. 'What's the matter? You look very flushed.'

'I'm all right. I thought it was later than it really was and I hurried back.' Then, to distract her aunt, she enquired, 'What did Fred Deeds mean when he talked about eating twelve grapes at midnight?'

'Didn't I tell you about that? At the first stroke of twelve, you start eating grapes — one for each month. If you manage to eat twelve before the clock stops striking it means you'll have good luck in the coming year. Of course it means you have to eat the pips as well.'

'I'll do my best. I could do with some good luck.'

Kathy and her aunt had been known to wash and change for dinner in ten minutes flat but preparation this evening was a long, slow ritual. Scented baths replaced hasty showers, hair was washed and styled and make-up was applied with careful attention to detail. Aunt Claudia was ready first and looked to Kathy for comments.

'You look marvellous,' her niece said sincerely.

'You mean for my age?'

'I mean for any age. David will have to fight off all the other men.'

Then Kathy sat in her slip while her aunt piled her bright hair on top of her head, allowing a few tendrils to frame her face.

Kathy stepped into her grey dress, her aunt zipped it up and Kathy turned round.

'How do I look?'

Her aunt did not reply immediately, and Kathy saw that she was blinking back tears.

'You look utterly beautiful. I wish you were my daughter. I wish your mother could see you now.'

Kathy took her hands and kissed her cheek.

'You would have made a wonderful mother. Now, shall we go down and dazzle Uncle David?'

'It is a pity you haven't got a partner for the night,' remarked her aunt as they left the room. 'Didn't you hope to see that nice young man, Miguel?'

'He had to go away and I gather he won't be able to get here tonight.'

Kathy was only human and it was very pleasant to be young and know that you look your very best, to sweep into the lounge and watch everybody turn to look at you and see the admiration grow on their faces. She forgot everything but the night ahead and David, who was looking very spruce himself, was glowing with smug pride as he settled the two of them on a couch.

'The head waiter said that we would start taking our seats at eight-thirty, so I'll get us all a drink to start the evening off.'

While she and Aunt Claudia waited for him to return, Kathy saw Elena Marquez walk through the lounge on some errand. Excusing herself, she hurried after the girl.

'Elena!'

The assistant manager turned. Although there were still shadows under her eyes she looked more composed than the last time Kathy had seen her.

'Elena, I just wanted to say how glad I am that everything has turned out all right.'

The Spanish girl's smooth brow wrinkled.

'All right? I don't understand.'

'I saw your brother on his way here today. I assumed he was coming to make his peace with you and make a fresh start.'

Elena's fingers gripped Kathy's arm.

'You saw him today? But he hasn't come here! Where did you see him?'

Kathy wished she hadn't said anything to rouse the girl's hopes.

'I saw him this morning very near the

hotel. At least, I think it was him.'

Elena shook her head regretfully.

'I am afraid you must have been mistaken. I haven't heard from him since I saw you last.'

'I'm sorry,' Kathy said helplessly.

The Spanish girl smiled.

'It was kind of you to think of me. I keep remembering what you said and hoping that he will see sense and come back to me.'

There was a movement among the guests in the lounge and Kathy heard her aunt call her name.

'I must go,' she said hurriedly. 'I hope it does turn out all right. When he does appear, tell him off for causing you so much worry.'

9

The doors to the dining-room had been
thrown open. For this one night of the
year the informal buffet dinner had
been abandoned and guests were led to
their seats.

As well as David and Aunt Claudia,
Kathy shared a table with Mrs Simmonds, Mrs Heswall and a shy elderly
gentleman.

The chef had been delighted at the
chance to show off his skills and had
produced a memorable meal, starting
with fish soup and followed by prawn
cocktails served in hollowed-out pine-
apples. Next came some superb beef
and then the meal finished with a
delicate creamy dessert. Anybody who
was still hungry could nibble almond
sweetmeats and dried fruits and by each
plate was a small serving of twelve
grapes.

It was a splendid dinner and everyone was thoroughly enjoying themselves. The shy man blossomed under the attentions of Mrs Simmonds and Mrs Heswall, Aunt Claudia and David were unashamedly holding hands when they were not toasting each other and Kathy felt that her holiday was having a very happy ending.

It was nearly ten o'clock when they returned to the lounge. The band began to play and people who had been announcing that they were so full of food they probably wouldn't be able to move all evening suddenly found that perhaps they could manage a dance or two.

David and Aunt Claudia were the first couple on the dance floor. Many of the other guests knew of their recent engagement and there was a spontaneous round of applause.

Patrick, very smart in a dinner jacket, appeared from nowhere and asked Kathy to dance.

'Doesn't everyone look splendid?'

Kathy said happily.

'Are you fishing for compliments?'

'Of course not!'

'You don't need to. You look very beautiful, Kathy.'

There was a warmth in his voice which brought the colour to her cheeks, but she smiled up at him mischievously.

'Don't they make striped dinner jackets?'

There was always someone eager to dance with Kathy, and finally she felt in need of brief respite and sought refuge in the cloakroom, where she refreshed her lipstick and checked that her hair had not collapsed. Instead of going straight back to her party, she slipped outside to the swimming pool area for a breath of fresh air.

Once outside, she could see the dancers through the big lounge windows and she was looking for her aunt's rose-pink dress when someone spoke close by her.

'Kathy!'

All she heard was her name, but that

was enough. She turned towards the direction of the voice.

'Kathy?' she queried. 'I thought Miss Brandon had become the suitable way to address me. From you, I think I would prefer Miss Brandon.'

Miguel stepped out of the shadows. In the light from the windows she saw that he was still wearing the black sweatshirt and jeans that she had seen him in earlier. His face was pale and set.

'Kathy, I know how much I must have hurt you the other evening and that you think I behaved badly but there was a reason for what I did.'

She waited, silent and unmoving, and he sighed and shook his head.

'I can't explain tonight. Tomorrow, perhaps, I will be able to tell you everything.'

'Tomorrow, perhaps? Perhaps when I am safely on the plane and you needn't worry about explanations to silly girls who amused you for a day or two.'

'That's not true!'

There was hurt anger in his tone.

'I would tell you now if I could but I promised other people that I would keep silent. Believe me, it is very important that I keep this secret for a few hours more. Please, trust me. Don't you feel you know me well enough to give me the benefit of the doubt?'

He came closer to her.

'Kathy, I told you a week ago that I would try to be here with you on New Year's Eve. Even earlier this evening I didn't think I would be able to get away but at the last moment I found that I was free, so I'm here — late and unsuitably dressed — but here because I want to be with you. In an hour's time this year will end. Can't we be together till then?'

Wounded pride, even common sense, told her to send him away. But this evening was removed from real time, an enchanted moment that might vanish with the stroke of midnight and she could think about common sense then. Kathy held out her hands to him and smiled.

'Dance with me,' she whispered.

Still holding hands, cherishing the contact, they entered the lounge and threaded their way through to the dance floor.

Aunt Claudia, dancing with her fiancé, saw them come in.

'She told me that he'd gone away!' she exclaimed.

David followed her gaze.

'Well, he's obviously made an effort and come back. I wonder why he's dressed like that? He's usually very smartly dressed.'

Other people looked at Miguel's sweatshirt and jeans but he and Kathy were oblivious to critical or approving looks. They were aware only of the warm nearness of each other, of the feel of each other's body moving to the rhythm of the dance.

'This is what I have been dreaming of for a week,' he murmured, 'and this is better than my dreams. You are very beautiful, Kathy Brandon.'

She smiled up at him.

'I'd given up dreaming. That is why this seems so wonderful.' She gave a little laugh. 'Are you going to abandon me at midnight again, as you did on Christmas Day?'

He held her closer.

'I intend to be here with you at midnight, to dance with you until the band refuses to play any more, and hopefully watch the sun rise with you.'

She sighed happily and Aunt Claudia, watching her with an expert's eye, nodded with satisfaction.

'I don't know whether this is a serious affair or whether she'll never see him again after tomorrow, but at least she is having one of those perfect evenings you remember all your life.'

'Just as I am,' David Evans said fondly and was rewarded with a kiss.

'Thirty minutes to midnight,' Miguel murmured in Kathy's ear. 'Have you got your twelve grapes?'

'They're on our table with Aunt Claudia's. What about you?'

He smiled into her eyes.

'I seem to be getting all the good luck I need.'

He looked round the dance floor and the crowded tables with a professional eye.

'It looks as if almost all the guests are here. The evening is definitely a success.'

She glanced round as well, glad that other people were happy as well on that special night.

'Fred Deeds isn't back yet,' she remarked.

'Fred Deeds?'

She felt a momentary tension in his body.

'He wasn't here for the Christmas Day dance because he's an ardent fisherman but I heard him tell some women that he would be back before midnight today.'

He stopped dancing abruptly and took her by the shoulders.

'Are you sure? We were informed he would come back in the morning. What exactly did he say?'

Shaken and confused, she stared at him.

'Does it matter? Who was informed?' she asked.

'What did he say?'

She responded to the urgency in his voice, frowning as she tried to recall the builder's exact words.

'He said that his plans were changed and that he would be back in time to see us eat our twelve grapes.'

His hands dropped from her and he whirled round and quickly made for the door.

Her dream suddenly changed to a nightmare, Kathy stood abandoned on the dance floor.

Aunt Claudia hurried swiftly to her side.

'What happened?'

Kathy allowed her aunt to guide her back to the table, blinking back tears.

'I don't know. We were talking about the guests and I mentioned Fred Deeds . . . '

Her eyes widened in horror and her hand went to her mouth. Several disparate items of information clicked into place to form a coherent picture in her mind.

There was Fred Deeds, out at night in a small boat and returning with a heavy box, the police at the hotel, and Elena Marquez's brother lurking in the nearby streets.

Kathy turned to her aunt.

'It's all right! I know what's the matter!'

The group of elderly faces looked at her with kind concern. She couldn't get them involved.

'Please, stay here! I've just got to make a call.'

She gathered up her grey skirts and made for the door. Her aunt hesitated, obviously about to follow but David placed a restraining hand on her arm.

'Let her go,' he advised. 'If it's trouble between lovers it's always best to let them sort it out by themselves,' and Aunt Claudia reluctantly sat down.

Out in the foyer Kathy saw only Patrick and Jane, a single couple dancing by themselves over the empty floor. She ran to them and they halted. Patrick looked concerned, but there was anger on Jane's face.

'Please!' Kathy exclaimed. 'It's an emergency!'

Automatically the two reps turned anxiously towards the lounge but Kathy clutched at them to restrain them.

'No! Nothing's happened in there. Fred Deeds is a drug smuggler and Miguel Lawrence has gone to look for him. But he doesn't know that Elena Marquez's brother is waiting to kill Deeds!'

Even as she spoke she was aware of how ridiculous and melodramatic she sounded. What proof had she got?

'Calm down, Kathy,' Patrick said soothingly, while Jane looked on stony-faced. 'What makes you think this?'

She clasped her hands together in entreaty.

'Deeds brings in drugs in his fishing

gear. I think Miguel has been helping the police look for the smuggler. That's why they were here the other day. Miguel didn't know that Deeds had altered his plans for tonight and will be back any minute. Probably the police hope to catch him with the drugs on him tonight. Juan Marquez also knows he is bringing in drugs and he plans to kill him to avenge his friends who died because of taking drugs.'

It still sounded unlikely but, as a travel rep, Patrick had had considerable experience in deciding when someone was speaking the truth.

'Jane, call the police,' he instructed with quiet efficiency. 'Kathy, do you know where they are likely to be?'

Kathy recalled her sightings of Deeds and Juan Marquez.

'To the left. There is a short cut from the fishing boats to the hotel some-where among those alleys by the shops.'

Patrick strode towards the front door, Kathy close behind him. He gestured to her to go back to Jane but Kathy shook her head with grim determination and followed him out into the night.

Music and laughter spilled out from houses and restaurants as the minutes to midnight ticked away, but the alleys and shops were dark and silent. Patrick hesitated.

'You go along the outside by the sea wall,' he ordered her. 'I'll go up and down these alleys. If you see anyone, shout out. Don't try and do anything brave by yourself.'

He slipped quietly into a nearby gaping entrance.

Kathy, left by herself, knew that he was trying to protect her by leaving her in the open and was suddenly overcome by fear. She was used to an orderly, peaceful life. What was she doing combing through the alleys in Majorca for hardened criminals at nearly midnight?

She wanted to run back to the brightly lit hotel and to the safety of her aunt's arms. Instead, she took a deep breath and hurried to the next dark gap showing the entrance to a narrow alley and peered down it. There was only silent darkness and no sign of movement. It was the same with the next entrance and the next.

Then from somewhere nearby she heard the sound of a scuffle and a scream and halted abruptly.

The walls of the nearby buildings echoed all sounds so that it was difficult to decide which direction the noise came from.

Kathy began to run, peering desperately down every opening. Was that Patrick she had heard screaming? If so, perhaps she was no longer the hunter but the hunted, with a ruthless enemy watching her run towards him. To conceal herself she ran down the next dark alley, then turned into the next. It was like a dreadful nightmare where she was trapped in a maze, terrified of some unknown threat.

Suddenly she heard the thud of blows, the rapid scrape of feet on the ground and gasping breaths as two men struggled with each other.

Round the next corner she turned she saw two figures locked in battle, silhouetted against the flickering neon sign of an advertisement. It was like watching a badly-projected film but she saw enough to realise that Patrick had found Fred Deeds and, as the two men swayed back and forth in combat, she realised that a third anonymous figure lay huddled on the ground.

Patrick had had the advantage of surprise but he was slighter than the builder, with no experience of street fighting and, as Kathy watched, she saw Deeds hit Patrick, who fell groaning on the floor. Deeds bent over him, pulling something from his jacket.

At that moment, Kathy heard the sound of someone else running towards them just before she felt herself thrust aside as none other than Miguel hurled himself at the drug smuggler.

Deeds swung round, swift as a cat, as

the running footsteps gave him warning, but Miguel was fast enough to catch him off balance. He recovered instantly, however, and the neon lights behind him flashed on the blade of the knife that he had drawn as he stooped over Patrick. Miguel feinted to the left and tried to close on Deeds and seize his wrist but Deeds was faster. Kathy saw the lifted knife curve forward with dreadful speed into Miguel's breast and then withdraw. Miguel fell to his knees.

Kathy was not aware that she had moved but somehow she was throwing herself at Deeds, clawing at his arm as he lifted the knife to strike again.

Almost casually he threw her aside so that she hit the wall but she stayed upright and launched herself at him again. The knife caught for a second in her dress skirt and she seized him and clung on as he viciously tried to shake her off.

Kathy saw Miguel, still on his knees, reach out and clamp his arms round Deeds' knees just as the builder managed to dislodge her and throw her back against the wall with such force that she slithered down it, half-stunned. Then, as the sound of bells marked midnight and the coming of New Year, Majorca seemed to explode in a pattern of bright lights and explosions.

As she lost consciousness, Kathy saw the alley suddenly fill with armed men in olive-green uniforms.

10

Kathy woke very reluctantly the next morning. She felt sore and stiff and her head was aching. She groaned.

'Kathy!'

Her aunt's voice roused her. She opened her eyes reluctantly and saw Aunt Claudia standing over her, her face tense with anxiety.

'Kathy! Wake up and tell me that you are all right!'

'My head hurts,' Kathy complained.

Her aunt vanished but soon reappeared with a cup of black coffee and some aspirins. She watched wordlessly as Kathy struggled upright and gratefully began to drink the coffee but as soon as it was finished Aunt Claudia broke into speech.

'What happened last night? First of all you vanished after that young man left you in the middle of the dance floor and then there was no sign of you till well after midnight. Then two policemen appeared almost carrying you and said that you'd had a bump on the head but a doctor had looked at you and had given you something to make you sleep, and said that all you needed was rest. They helped me bring you up here and then left without saying any more. I've been worrying myself sick all night while you just slept. What happened?'

Kathy frowned.

'I feel all muzzy, I can't think straight,' she complained.

Her aunt tried again, her voice carefully controlled.

'Kathy Brandon, you were brought back last night by the police after someone hit you. Your beautiful dress is ruined. It is torn and it's got blood on it. In addition, it is nearly ten o'clock, I haven't had any breakfast, and we are supposed to have packed and left this room by twelve. What am I going to tell your mother?'

The last sentence came out on a

high, almost hysterical note. Aunt Claudia was losing control.

Kathy was sitting bolt upright now, scenes from the previous night flashing through her brain.

'There was blood on my dress?'

She suddenly remembered a flash-back of a knife aimed at Miguel's kneeling figure.

'Aunt Claudia, what happened?'

'That is what I am asking you!' her aunt snapped.

At that moment the telephone rang.

Aunt Claudia snatched it up and Kathy saw her aunt listen intently and then relax.

'That would be very kind of you. Orange juice, scrambled eggs on toast, and coffee,' her aunt listed, and then put the phone down.

'I don't know why,' she said rather wearily, 'but that was reception offering to have breakfast sent up for us. They also said that we can stay in our room all afternoon if we like, and they will send us to the airport in a taxi.' She

165

turned on Kathy like a tigress. 'Do you remember anything yet?'

'Give me five minutes,' Kathy pleaded, and stumbled to the bathroom to clean her teeth and splash water on her face.

Looking in the mirror, she groaned at the white face, still smeared with make-up from the previous night. There were dark shadows under her eyes, and her hair looked like a bird's nest.

A tap on the door announced that breakfast had been delivered and, by mutual unspoken consent, both aunt and niece put other matters aside until they had eaten.

Afterwards, Kathy told Aunt Claudia what she could remember and what had led up to the previous night. She saw her aunt's lips tighten when she revealed that she had spent two separate days with Miguel without telling her aunt.

'Patrick was hurt, I know, and so was Miguel.' She went on. 'I don't know how badly, however, and I don't know who the other man was on the ground. I must find out!'

'Why don't you have a bath while I go downstairs and see if I can discover anything?' her aunt suggested. 'I must find David, anyway. He was terribly worried when you were brought back last night.'

Kathy was grateful for the warm bath soothing her bruised body. She dried herself slowly and carefully, wincing as she touched unsuspected tender spots, and then washed her hair under the shower.

When she opened the wardrobe to get out something to wear, she saw her grey dress in a pile on the floor. Her aunt had been right. It was dirty, torn and bloodstained — beyond recovery. It had been the most beautiful dress she had ever possessed but reluctantly she put it in the waste bin.

She chose a simple cream cotton dress to wear. With her damp hair hanging straight to her shoulders and with her face innocent of a trace of make-up, she looked about sixteen. When there was a knock on the door she went to open it, assuming that it was Aunt Claudia.

It was Miguel!

They looked at each other with relief.

'You're alive!' Kathy managed.

'And I'm glad to see you don't look too badly hurt,' he replied.

Miguel stepped into the room and closed the door behind him. In the bright light from the window Kathy could see that he was haggard and pale and still in last night's clothes, which now looked dusty and torn. There was no sign of the elegant young business-man about him now.

'I came to thank you for saving my life,' he said gravely. 'If you hadn't hung on to Deed's arm he would have stabbed me again.'

'I had to help,' she began, starting towards him, but he backed away almost in alarm, holding his hands before him defensively. She looked at him in indignant surprise, and he lifted the edge of his sweatshirt sufficiently for her to see the edge of a large white dressing which covered half of his chest.

'Kathy, last week I promised myself that I would kiss you at midnight on New Year's Eve,' he said. 'Mr Deeds put paid to that plan and if you touch me now I'll probably curl up and die.'

'Is that where he stabbed you? Is it a bad wound?'

'Comparatively speaking it's not too bad. It's not very deep and it was clean, so it hasn't put me in hospital, anyway. But it definitely hurts a lot!'

'Sit here,' she instructed him, guiding him to the armchair by the window. 'There's some coffee in the pot, though it's probably cold by now.'

'I don't care whether it's hot or cold,' he replied and took the cup in both hands, draining it gratefully.

'Haven't you had any sleep?' she demanded.

He shook his head slowly.

'There were too many things to do, too many loose ends to tidy up.'

'What happened after Deeds knocked me out?'

'We managed to give each other a couple of punches and then the Guardia Civil arrived. A group of them were not far away. They were supposed to go down to the harbour later and seize Deeds before he could land and get rid of the drugs but, as you told me, he'd changed his plans. When the police station got Jane's call they came charging down and Deeds didn't stand a chance. He's safely locked up now, charged with smuggling drugs, attempted murder and a few other things.'

Relief swept through her at his last sentence.

'Only attempted murder. So Patrick is all right?'

'He's covered with bruises and is at his flat being nursed by Jane. The company's rushed another rep in to look after things.'

'And the other man, the one on the ground?'

'Juan Marquez, who is very lucky indeed to be alive,' Miguel said grimly. 'He attacked Deeds but he never had a chance and was badly beaten up. I heard the whole story from Elena at about two o'clock this morning.'

'What will happen to him?'

He smiled reassuringly.

'The Guardia Civil have been assured that Juan saw a man acting suspiciously and tackled him. The police will be quite content to accept that. They don't want to bother with a silly boy who has assured his sister that he's seen the error of his ways. If he needs any help in the way of treatment at a clinic I'll see he gets it. Elena is a valuable employee.'

His eyes were drooping, but he forced them open.

'I think that if you bent over me very carefully, I might manage that kiss now.'

'Certainly not,' she said firmly. 'Anyway, a few days ago you didn't want anything to do with me. Can you tell me why now?'

'Can't you guess? We were pretty sure that Deeds was the man we wanted, and then in you walked, arm in arm with him and carrying a bag full of drugs! The officer was convinced that you were an accomplice. He forbade me to speak to you again until he'd had you checked out. I knew you were innocent but I didn't want Deeds to know that we were friends in case he thought I was using you to spy on him. If you remember, he was in the foyer later when you came to speak to me.'

She nodded thoughtfully and there was a pause, and then there was another tap on the door and this time it was Aunt Claudia.

She bustled in, highly excited, and then stopped at the sight of Miguel. His head was thrown back and his eyes were closed. He had finally given in to the overwhelming need for sleep.

Kathy dragged a blanket off the bed and tucked it round him. She looked down at him for a moment and then took her aunt by the arm.

'I think we'd better find somewhere else to talk.'

They went downstairs and for the first time Kathy realised that the New Year was starting with a beautiful day.

They went to join David on the sun terrace and, when Kathy appeared, a number of interested faces turned towards her.

'Of course, they saw you being carried in last night,' her aunt said, and promptly busied herself warding off all those who thought Kathy might be able to shed light on the mysterious events of the previous night. She was polite but firm and all the interested parties retreated in defeat.

'You can't blame them,' she told her companions when they had finally been left by themselves. 'First there was you and then Mr Lawrence practically staggered in, apparently dripping blood all over the place. There were telephone calls going on to the police and to hospitals and finally some people who'd gone outside to see what was happening came back and said Mr Deeds had been dragged into a police van and taken away.'

She stopped and looked at Kathy hopefully.

'Did that young man have a chance to tell you anything before he fell asleep?'

Kathy gave her the extra information she had gathered from Miguel.

Aunt Claudia and David listened spellbound.

'So Patrick got hurt as well and Jane is looking after him,' Aunt Claudia said thoughtfully. 'Well, it was obvious that she liked him but, of course, he hadn't noticed. This will give her a chance to show how loving and caring she can be.'

'What happens now?' David asked.

'I'd like to go for lunch,' Kathy said firmly. 'All the excitement seems to have made me very hungry.'

They returned to the same restaurant as the previous day for a long farewell lunch.

'We'll have to pack soon,' her aunt

sighed after they had eaten. 'It's two o'clock now and the plane flies at six. Even if we go by taxi we'll have to leave the hotel by half-past four at the latest.'

'It's difficult to believe that in four hours time we will be leaving Majorca behind us,' David commented. 'It has been a most unusual and exciting holiday.'

Looking at him, Kathy realised that he was thinking primarily of his engagement to Aunt Claudia. As for the rest, his future niece by marriage and a few young men had had a nasty brush with a criminal but there had been no lasting harm done. He would look back on it, from the security of a happy marriage, as a minor incident. Well, she supposed it put everything into perspective.

When they returned to their room, the armchair was empty and the blanket neatly folded on the bed.

Kathy realised with an awful sinking feeling that she might never see Miguel again. He had thanked her for coming to his aid and told her what had happened to those involved. There was no reason why he should seek her out again in the few hours which now remained. He had gone without the kiss he had promised himself but would he really mind that much?

The two women started to complete their packing, but the telephone's insistent ringing interrupted them and Kathy picked it up.

'It's the police,' she told her aunt. 'They are at the hotel and they'd like me to make a statement.'

'I can finish the packing for both of us,' her aunt assured her. 'Go and give your statement so that we have some chance of leaving on time.'

Kathy found the police in a large office on the first floor. She was naturally nervous at first but they were polite and reassuring. It was not as if her evidence was particularly important. Deeds had been found with drugs in his possession and trying to kill Miguel. The case against him was watertight. Kathy simply told them briefly how she and Patrick had followed Miguel when he had rushed out of the hotel and had got involved in his pursuit with Deeds. She did not say a word about Juan Marquez.

'I think that is all, Miss Brandon,' the senior officer said politely. 'If you will just wait here, I will check that you are not needed for anything else.'

The two policemen left Kathy alone in the room and she waited for their return without anxiety. She had full confidence in Aunt Claudia's ability to finish the packing and organise the collection of their luggage. In the peaceful sun-filled room she closed her eyes and began to drift off to sleep, until the door opening and closing roused her. Instead of the policeman it was Miguel, clean and freshly dressed in a white shirt and dark trousers.

'Don't get up,' he instructed. 'I know just how you feel.'

He leaned against the desk and smiled down at her.

'The police have asked me to convey their thanks for your co-operation and tell you that you are free to go. The taxi for the airport will be here in half an hour.'

Was that all? Wasn't he even going to say goodbye? Apparently not, for as she rose he went to open the door for her. Suddenly she saw him wince and her attempt at a dignified exit was forgotten immediately.

'Are you still in pain?' she said anxiously. 'Shouldn't you go back to the hospital?'

He moved his shoulder uneasily, and his grin looked a little strained.

'It hurts when I lift my arm, that's all. I'm not sure how I'm going to put my jacket on but I won't need that until we are on the plane.'

'The plane?' Kathy repeated bewilderedly.

'I'm coming back to England with you, for a few days at least. My mother will be waiting at the airport, incidentally. She is very eager to meet her

178

future daughter-in-law.'

The world seemed to whirl round Kathy. She sat down again abruptly

'Her future daughter-in-law?'

He lifted surprised eyebrows.

'Of course. You did save my life. You know very well that in the old stories if a prince rescued a damsel in distress he always married her. In these days of sexual equality, if a girl rescues a man she has to marry him. My mother agreed with this, especially when I told her that I fell in love with you the third time I met you.'

Kathy's main emotion, surpassing even her surprised delight and happiness, was sheer anger.

'You never told me that! You never told me that you loved me! You let me fret in case you were just using me to amuse yourself with in your spare time, in case it was just a holiday romance!'

He gazed at her with apparently genuine amazement.

'But, Kathy, did I have to say it? Wasn't it obvious?'

As she glared at him, he bent forward.

'Will this convince you?'

It was a long, gentle and loving kiss.

'I'm sorry,' he said apologetically when it finally finished. 'This is the first time I have ever loved anyone like this. I don't know what to say or do so I'm probably making a fool of myself.'

Kathy made a gigantic effort to pull herself together and get back to the real world.

'This is silly! You say you love me and I think I love you but we've only known each other for a few days on a holiday island. When we get back to England we may find that we have nothing in common, that we annoy each other or even bore each other.'

'Do you think that is likely?' he said softly, and she had no reply.

This time it was not a tap but a very determined knock on the door, followed by the immediate entrance of Aunt Claudia, with David in attendance.

'Kathy, we will be leaving soon!'

'It's all right, Aunt Claudia. We are both coming now.'

As they left the room Aunt Claudia eyed Miguel with interest.

'You look a bit better than you did this morning.'

'I'm recovering quickly, and my mother will be at the airport in England, so she will look after me from then on.'

'Really?' Aunt Claudia looked sideways at her niece. 'I wonder if she'll meet your mother, Kathy?'

Kathy stared at her and her aunt looked a little defensive.

'Well, I thought I ought to warn her what's been happening. I knew they got back a couple of days ago so I telephoned her while you were with the police. She said she would meet the plane.'

'Those wedding plans will have been finalised by the time we reach England,' Miguel whispered to Kathy.

She bit her lip.

'I haven't agreed to marry you yet, Miguel. I want to be wooed and to be courted properly. I want to be persuaded, gradually, that I might possibly at some time consider you as a husband.'

She got into the waiting taxi.

'And then you'll say yes,' Miguel murmured as he prepared to follow her. 'Happy New Year, Kathy!'

THE END

We do hope that you have enjoyed reading this large print book.

Did you know that all of our titles are available for purchase?

We publish a wide range of high quality large print books including:
Romances, Mysteries, Classics
General Fiction
Non Fiction and Westerns

Special interest titles available in large print are:
The Little Oxford Dictionary
Music Book, Song Book
Hymn Book, Service Book

Also available from us courtesy of Oxford University Press:
Young Readers' Dictionary
(large print edition)
Young Readers' Thesaurus
(large print edition)

For further information or a free brochure, please contact us at:
Ulverscroft Large Print Books Ltd.,
The Green, Bradgate Road, Anstey,
Leicester, LE7 7FU, England.
Tel: (00 44) **0116 236 4325**
Fax: (00 44) **0116 234 0205**

*Other titles in the
Linford Romance Library:*

VISIONS OF THE HEART

Christine Briscomb

When property developer Connor
Grant contracted Natalie Jensen to
landscape the grounds of his large
country house near Ashley in South
Australia, she was ecstatic. But then
she discovered he was acquiring
— and ripping apart — great
swathes of the town. Her own
mother's house and the hall where
the drama group met were two of his
targets. Natalie was desperate to
stop Connor's plans — but she also
had to fight the powerful attraction
flowing between them.